Reunion

A Musical Epic in Miniature

Book by
Jack Kyrieleison

Story by
Jack Kyrieleison
and ### Ron Holgate

Traditional Music Arranged by
Michael O'Flaherty

A SAMUEL FRENCH ACTING EDITION

SAMUEL
FRENCH

FOUNDED 1830

NEW YORK HOLLYWOOD LONDON TORONTO

SAMUELFRENCH.COM

RENTAL MATERIALS

An orchestration consisting of a **Piano/Conductor Score**, and addional parts for **Violin, Trumpet, Banjo/Guitar, Bass and Percussion** will be loaned two months prior to the production ONLY on the receipt of the Licensing Fee quoted for all performances, the rental fee and a refundable deposit.

Please contact Samuel French for perusal of the music materials as well as a performance license application.

IMPORTANT BILLING AND CREDIT REQUIREMENTS

All producers of *REUNION must* give credit to the Author of the Play in all programs distributed in connection with performances of the Play, and in all instances in which the title of the Play appears for the purposes of advertising, publicizing or otherwise exploiting the Play and/or a production. The name of the Author *must* appear on a separate line on which no other name appears, immediately following the title and *must* appear in size of type not less than fifty percent of the size of the title type.

REUNION opened at Theatre Row in New York on March 26, 1999. The show opened as a production of AMAS Musical Theatre, and was subsequently produced commercially by Eugene Kallman, with Donna Trinkoff as the Associate Producer. The production was directed by Ron Holgate. The set designer was Doug Huszti, the costume designer was Jan Finnell, the lighting designer was Stephen Petrilli, with publicity by Tony Origlio, and casting by Donna DeSeta Casting. The production stage manager was Carlos A. Mongé, III and William Repicci served as the general manager. Musical Direction by Robert Lamont, with orchestrations by Andrew Wilder and musical staging by Karen Azenberg. The cast was as follows:

MR. HARRY HAWK	Joe Barrett
MR. TOM TRUDGETT	Don Burroughs
MISS CORDELIA HOPEWELL	Donna Lynne Champlin
MRS. CASSIE DRUMWRIGHT	Harriett D. Foy
MR. AUGUSTIN LOVECRAFT	Jonathan Hadley
MR. HANNIBAL DRUMWRIGHT	Michael A. Shepperd

MUSICIANS

Musical Director/Piano	Robert Lamont
Percussion	Joseph Brady
Guitar-Banjo	Robert Braunstein
Violin	Cody Ritchey
Trumpet	Dan Yeager

REUNION was originally produced in 1996 as *BATTLE CRY OF FREEDOM* for The Goodspeed Opera House by Michael P. Price, Executive Producer.

CHARACTERS AND CASTING

(4 males, 2 females)

REUNION was written to be performed by 6 actor/singers but can be expanded to virtually any size. It has been staged very effectively with 28 performers and there is no reason it could not accommodate as many as a group has available. There are two options for expanding the cast:

Assign the major acting roles to the 6 principals as in the standard script and assign a group of performers (minimum 1 woman and 2 men) as Ensemble for supporting roles and as a self-contained group of music hall performers for the songs *Darling Nelly Gray, Abraham's Daughter, Pat Murphy of the Irish Brigade, Der Deitcher's Dog,* and *Grafted into the Army.* (This will also help to distribute rehearsal time, as one group can rehearse musical numbers while the other rehearses scene work.)

OR

Reassign all roles using the Expanded Cast breakdown.

If the cast size is enlarged much beyond 6, Harry Hawk's introductory speech should be replaced by the alternate version included at the back of the script to justify so many performers being available to the cash-strapped impresario.

ABOUT THE CHARACTERS

MR. HARRY HAWK – Middle-aged, company leading man and manager. Baritone. Plays Union general George McClellan, John Wilkes Booth, a music hall comedian and several smaller roles. Hawk is a resourceful survivor who has talked his way out of more than a few tight places, not the least of which was the interrogation he endured in the Old Capitol Prison the night Lincoln was assassinated. With the vanity of the Victorian actor-manager, he has reserved the most flamboyant role for himself, even though a good many years past his prime. But where others might notice an expanding paunch or a receding hairline, when Hawk looks in the mirror a virile young hero still stares back at him.

MR. AUGUSTIN LOVECRAFT – Late 20s-early 30s. The company's light comedian. High baritone. Plays Lincoln's secretary, an Irish tenor, and several smaller roles. Lovecraft is the most sophisticated member of the company and isn't shy about showing it. As a rising young actor, Lovecraft embraces a more modern, subtler style than the declamatory Harry Hawk. The natural rivalry between them should occasionally spill over to their interactions with each other during the play, allowing each to enjoy it that much more when his character scores a point at the other's expense.

MR. HANNIBAL DRUMWRIGHT – Middle-aged, African-American. Company stage manager. Bass-baritone. Plays a fugitive slave turned freedman and several smaller roles. Hannibal and Hawk have travelled together for a quarter of a century and have become so interdependent onstage and off that it's hard to imagine one without the other. As Hawk's stage manager, Hannibal keeps things running and there is no onstage emergency he has not had to find a way out of.

MRS. CASSIE DRUMWRIGHT – Middle-aged, African-American. Company wardrobe mistress. Mezzo. Plays a slave turned Underground Railroad guide, an elegant Washington freedwoman and several smaller roles. Married to Hannibal, Cassie is part of Hawk's company not out of a love of theatre, but because she chooses to go where Hannibal goes. Observant, practical and unsentimental, she takes life as she finds it and has little interest in the self-absorption of actors or the dramatics of their interpersonal relationships. Both she and Hannibal have been pressed into service onstage as the company's failing economic fortunes have made it necessary.

MISS CORDELIA HOPEWELL – 20s. Company ingenue. Soprano. Plays a romantic small-town girl, a New England abolitionist turned volunteer nurse, a music hall performer, and several smaller roles. Cordelia is a creature of the theatre and wrings every available ounce of romance out of it. And though it secretly pleases her to be thought of as the jewel of Hawk's company, she is sweet-natured enough not to use that status any more than absolutely necessary.

MR. TOM TRUDGETT – Late teens or 20s. Company juvenile. Tenor. Plays a young millworker who volunteers for the Union army, a music hall performer and several smaller roles. Not an actor by training or design, his appealing looks, sincerity, willingness to work and good nature, coupled with a search for adventure, have landed him in the midst of Hawk's company. He is generally in awe of his fellow actors, particularly Cordelia, and there are moments when he simply cannot believe his good fortune.

ALTERNATE BREAKDOWN FOR EXPANDED CAST PRODUCTIONS

The roles have been redistributed in this version to create opportunities for more performers. There are 12 principal roles (7m, 5f) and an ensemble of any size. If desired, 6 of the principals (see below) can be cast from the ensemble.

HARRY HAWK – Mature, baritone actor-manager. The company actor-manager plays himself, a flamboyant tragedian, and Union General George McClellan.

HANNIBAL DRUMWRIGHT – Mature, low baritone, African-American. The company stage manager plays himself, and a fugitive slave turned freedman in the North who volunteers as a Union soldier.

CASSIE DRUMWRIGHT – Mature, mezzo, African-American. The company wardrobe mistress plays herself, Underground Railroad Guide.

THE SECRETARY – Youthful, high baritone, sophisticated company comedian. Plays Lincoln's Secretary.

THE NURSE – Youthful, soprano, company leading lady/ingenue. Plays an abolitionist who volunteers as a Union nurse.

THE SOLDIER – Youthful, tenor, the company juvenile, the boy next door. Plays a young Northern millhand who volunteers as a Union soldier.

The following 6 roles can be cast from the ensemble if needed:

THE DRESSMAKER – Mature, mezzo, African-American.

THE HOMETOWN GIRL – Youthful, soprano, patriotic small-town girl.

MUSIC HALL PERFORMERS – 3M, 1F, appear as minstrel trio, dancers, Irish tenor, comedians.

ENSEMBLE ROLES (all doubled):

New Yorker 1	General Pope	Washingtonians
New Yorker 2	Recruit 1	Theatregoers
New Yorker 3	Recruit 2	New Yorkers
New Yorker 4	Recruit 3	Farewell Committee
Secessionist	Southern Officer	Music Hall Girls
Maid	Rioter	McClellan Admirers
Female Northern Spy	Union Soldier 1	Society Ladies
Newsboy	Union Soldier 2	Do-Gooders
Telegraph Clerk	Union Soldier 3	Union Supporters
Guard	John Wilkes Booth	Union Recruits
Temperance Lady	Mrs. Muzzy	Union Soldiers
Saloonkeeper	Laura Keene	Mourners
Union Picket		

ORCHESTRATION

6 pieces
(Piano/synthesizer, violin, trumpet, banjo/guitar, bass, percussion)

TIME

8 o'clock in the evening, April 14, 1890.

PLACE

A theatre.

The play is performed with one intermission.

AUTHORS' NOTES

REUNION is told through the eyes of those who took up the Union cause – an intersection of theatre and history, weaving together songs from the period, visual images and dialogue adapted directly from eyewitness accounts.

All songs date from the Civil War or before, and the dialogue is drawn from or inspired by accounts from scores of participants like Walt Whitman, Louisa May Alcott, Frederick Douglass, John Hay, Harriet Tubman, George McClellan, many Union soldiers, and, of course, Abraham Lincoln. Occasionally there are references to "magic lantern" projections of specific photographs – technology that was available and in use at the time the play is set. The projection cues in the stage directions should be viewed as a guide, and images of those projections are provided in the back of the script. But a production could include more or fewer or different projections as circumstances allow.

The show is a Victorian entertainment, presented by the fictional company of the actor-manager Harry Hawk. Hawk was a real actor of the period, and was indeed standing alone on stage performing for President Lincoln at the moment he was assassinated. However, Hawk's production and the other members of his "company" are invented. He embodies the virtues and excesses of rip-roaring, Eliza-crossing-the-ice 19th-Century stagecraft, and he's tried to pack it all into this show: music hall, Victorian sentiment, minstrel show, florid tragedy and patriotic pageant.

Each actor has a basic costume suggestive of his place in the company hierarchy. Individual costume pieces are added and subtracted – the changes are usually part of the action, which is pretty much nonstop.

Some kind of projection system is needed for displaying the "magic lantern" projections that accompany songs and scenes and are key to placing the events in historical context. The projections allow the show to work for an audience with little or no existing knowledge of the Civil War.

The cues for the "magic lantern" projections in the stage directions should be viewed as a guide and reflect what worked for previous audiences. Images for these projections are available from the publisher in digital form, but a producer should not feel confined to using only those images and could include more, fewer or different images as circumstances dictate. To obtain the projections used in the original performance, please contact Samuel French, Inc.

As for sets, ideally there is an act curtain. A well-worn placard in front of the curtain reads: "TO-NIGHT!!! SPECIAL ENGAGEMENT! MR. HARRY HAWK'S COMPANY! ONLY LOCAL APPEARANCE!" A unit set with a second level upstage would be useful. Behind that, a generic wall or exterior flats with enough open space for "magic lantern" projections to be displayed – the larger the better. On stage right, stock interior flats – the kind Victorian theatres kept on hand for touring companies – set with a practical door and practical window, the window at second-story level if possible. On stage left, stock exterior flats or ground row with an entrance opposite the door stage right. This will be draped with plain canvas midway through Act 1 to suggest a commander's field tent in the Civil War. Upstage near the "tent" is some sort of contraption used by Hannibal to reveal a large portrait of whichever Union general happens to be in command. It can be as elaborate as a crank-and-rope mechanical or as simple as a couple of nails to hold placards hung in place.

But Victorians loved stage machinery, so the more inventive the better. Seats and levels materialize from theatrical trunks, wardrobe hampers and whatever else is readily at hand. There are a few simple chairs available on the set or in the wings for placement by the actors when needed. This labor, like the other stagecraft chores, more often than not falls to Hannibal, Cassie and Trudgett. Victorian theatre trappings are encouraged: footlights, thunder sheets, wind machines, moving ground row panoramas – all things that Hawk's vagabonds might find on hand when they arrived at a typical 19th Century theatre.

Lighting is especially important and the more acting areas available to isolate scenes, the better. While many scenes are played realistically, others are meant to be theatrically presentational, including all of the "music hall" numbers and production numbers like "We'll Fight for Uncle Abe," which should be treated like a minstrel show cakewalk. Footlights are a great addition for the more theatrical scenes.

About the language: the dialogue in *REUNION* is virtually all adapted directly from words of actual participants in the events of the play. In some cases this means using controversial language that was freely used by both blacks and whites during the Civil War era, specifically the term "nigger." *REUNION* has been produced with and without the word and the writers believe strongly that, coming as it does from sources like Harriet Tubman, the play is much more powerful with the original language intact. However, we recognize that feelings about racial terms can also create an obstacle to performing the play. Each community and theatre needs to reflect on its own standards, and in cases where the term is felt to be too objectionable to use, the word "black" should be substituted.

–Jack Kyrieleison, Ron Holgate, Michael O'Flaherty

SONGS IN *REUNION*

"Darling Nelly Gray" by Benjamin R. Hanby

"The Liberty Ball" by Jesse Hutchinson

"Lincoln And Liberty" (Traditional)

"May God Save The Union" by Rev. G. Douglass Brewerton & Carl Wolfsohn

"Abraham's Daughter" by Septimus Winner

"Home, Sweet Home" by John Howard Payne & Henry R. Bishop

"Marching Along" by William R. Bradbury

"Comrades, Fill No Glass For Me" by Stephen Foster

"All Quiet Along The Potomac Tonight" by Ethel L. Beers & John Hill Hewitt

"We'll Fight For Uncle Abe" by C.E. Pratt & Frederick Buckley

"Better Times Are Coming" by Stephen Foster

"We Are Coming, Father Abr'am" by James Sloan Gibbons & L.O. Emerson

"Wake Nicodemus" by Henry Clay Work

"Pat Murphy Of The Irish Brigade" (Traditional)

"Wasn't That A Wide River" (Traditional)

"Battle Cry Of Freedom" by George F. Root

"Heav'n Bound Soldier" (Traditional)

"Der Deitcher's Dog" by Septimus Winner

"John Brown's Body" (Traditional)

"Somebody's Darling" by Marie Ravenal de la Coste & John Hill Hewitt

"Grafted Into The Army" by Henry Clay Work

"Weeping Sad And Lonely" by Charles C. Sawyer & Henry Tucker

"Tenting On The Old Camp Ground" by Walter F. Kittredge

"Marching Through Georgia" by Henry Clay Work

"Beautiful Dreamer" by Stephen Foster

"Steal Away" (Traditional)

"Hard Times Come Again No More" by Stephen Foster

All songs are in the public domain.

ACT I

*(House lights dim. A drumroll, a trumpet fanfare, and a spotlight. The act curtain lurches open to reveal **HARRY HAWK**, a down-at-the-heels actor/ manager, and four of his company – **CORDELIA HOPEWELL**, **TOM TRUDGETT**, and **CASSIE** and **HANNIBAL DRUMWRIGHT** – caught in a frantic effort to locate one of their number. After a deeply awkward moment they recognize they are in full view of the audience and abruptly compose themselves into a tableau behind **HAWK**. He addresses the audience with practiced charm.)*

HAWK. Distinguished patrons of the Lyceum! I welcome you this evening with a deep sense of occasion, for it is a quarter of a century to the day – indeed, almost to the hour – since I found myself center stage in the tragic drama that shook the republic to its very foundations. Permit me to introduce myself – Harry Hawk! Actor, manager – one might even say impresario of our wandering band! Tonight, it is our great honor to present the story of The Late War To Save The Union, woven from the very words of those engaged in that heroic struggle, bedecked with the never-to-be-forgotten melodies of those tempest-tossed years, and illuminated by the astonishing wonders of…The Magic Lantern!

(A triumphant chord from the orchestra. A projection appears on upstage wall:)

PROJECTION (1):
MR. HARRY HAWK'S
COMPANY PRESENTS
"REUNION!"
THE AMERICAN ILIAD!

(**HAWK** *continues grandly.*)

HAWK. *(cont.)* For the past quarter of a century, we have played our drama before the Great and the near-Great, the very stage itself bursting to hold our army of actors and the sheer extravagance of our production!

(He comes back down to earth.)

But unhappily, you find us in somewhat diminished circumstances, as a regrettable misunderstanding with certain of our less imaginative creditors has dictated the hasty withdrawal of our forces from the field of our latest triumph. It pains me to announce that in the chaos of retreat, not all of our brave number escaped. Ah, well. In the death-less words of Homer, "Surely these things lie in the lap of the gods. For there is –"

(But a supremely self-assured and unconcerned **AUGUSTIN LOVECRAFT**, *the final member of the company, chooses precisely this moment to stroll on. With a smile at the audience and a nod to* **HAWK**, *he stations himself prominently in the group.* **HAWK** *begins again, his icy gaze fixed on* **LOVECRAFT**, *with the resignation of a man who has survived many theatrical battles.)*

"For there is a strength in the union even of *very sorry men.*"

*(**HANNIBAL** coughs discreetly, and* **HAWK** *is instantly the gracious host once more.)*

Therefore, tonight each of us appears before you in many roles, asking only that you unfetter your imaginations as you journey with us. In the fervent hope that you shall deem us worthy of your approbation, I give you our musical epic – in miniature.

(With a deep bow, he exits. Blackout.)

> *PROJECTION (2):*
> *"MR. LOVECRAFT,*
> *MR. HAWK & MR. TRUDGETT IN*
> *'DARLING NELLY GRAY'"*

(Footlights up on **HAWK, LOVECRAFT & TRUD-GETT** *as* **MINSTREL TRIO.** *)*

MINSTREL 1 (LOVECRAFT).
THERE'S A LOW GREEN VALLEY
ON THE OLD KENTUCKY SHORE,
THERE I'VE WHILED MANY HAPPY HOURS AWAY,
A-SITTIN' AND A-SINGIN'
BY THE LITTLE COTTAGE DOOR
WHERE LIVED MY DARLING NELLY GRAY.

MINSTREL TRIO (HAWK, LOVECRAFT, TRUDGETT).
OH! MY POOR NELLY GRAY,
THEY HAVE TAKEN YOU AWAY
AND I'LL NEVER SEE MY DARLING ANY MORE.
I'M A-SITTIN' BY THE RIVER
AND I'M WEEPING ALL THE DAY,
FOR YOU'VE GONE FROM THE OLD KENTUCKY SHORE.

(Lights up on an impassioned **ABOLITIONIST (CORDELIA).** *She holds up a book, addressing a large unseen crowd. Music under.)*

> *PROJECTION (2.1):*
> *TITLE PAGE OF*
> *"UNCLE TOM'S CABIN"*

THE ABOLITIONIST (CORDELIA). Men and women of America, is slavery a thing to be defended, apologized for, passed over in silence? This Union will

THE ABOLITIONIST (CORDELIA). *(cont.)* not be saved by protecting slavery! For there is no stronger law than that by which injustice and cruelty shall bring on nations the wrath of Almighty God!

(Lights up on an **UNDERGROUND RAILROAD GUIDE (CASSIE)** *holding a lantern.)*

THE GUIDE (CASSIE). I think slavery is the next thing to hell! If a person would send another into bondage, he would, it appears to me, be bad enough to send him into hell, if he could.

MINSTREL TRIO.
WHEN THE MOON HAD CLIMBED THE MOUNTAIN
AND THE STARS WERE SHINING TOO,
THEN I'D TAKE MY DARLING NELLY GRAY,
AND WE'D FLOAT DOWN THE RIVER
IN MY LITTLE RED CANOE,
WHILE MY BANJO SWEETLY I WOULD PLAY.
OH! MY POOR NELLY GRAY,
THEY HAVE TAKEN YOU AWAY
AND I'LL NEVER SEE MY DARLING ANY MORE,
I'M A-SITTIN' BY THE RIVER
AND I'M WEEPING ALL THE DAY,
FOR YOU'VE GONE FROM THE OLD KENTUCKY
    SHORE...

*(*TRIO *hum under. Lights up on* FUGITIVE SLAVE (HANNIBAL)*.)*

THE FUGITIVE (HANNIBAL). I have fled to the highest hills of the forest, pressing my way to the North, but the river Ohio was my limit. It was an impassable gulf. Sometimes, standing on the Ohio River bluff, I gazed upon the blue sky of the free North and thought...

THE GUIDE. Oh, that I had the wings of a dove...

THE FUGITIVE. ...that I might soar away to where there is no slavery...

THE GUIDE. …no clanking of chains…

THE GUIDE & THE FUGITIVE. …no parting of husbands and wives….

*(Projection out. This verse is accompanied by maudlin, theatrical gestures from **THE MINSTRELS**, in contrast to **THE GUIDE** and **THE FUGITIVE**.)*

MINSTREL 1.

ONE NIGHT I WENT TO SEE HER
BUT "SHE'S GONE!" THE NEIGHBORS SAY,
THE WHITE MAN BOUND HER WITH HIS CHAIN.
THEY HAVE TAKEN HER TO GEORGIA
FOR TO WEAR HER LIFE AWAY,
AS SHE TOILS IN THE COTTON AND THE CANE…

THE FUGITIVE. …I thought of the fishes of the water,…

THE GUIDE. …the fowls of the air,…

THE FUGITIVE. …the wild beasts of the forest. All appeared to be free…

THE GUIDE. …to go just where they pleased….

(Music out.)

THE FUGITIVE. And I was an unhappy slave.

PROJECTION (3): POSTER –
"COLORED PEOPLE OF BOSTON!
BEWARE OF SLAVECATCHERS
AND KIDNAPPERS!"

MINSTREL 1.

OH! MY DARLING NELLY GRAY,
UP IN HEAVEN THERE THEY SAY,
THAT THEY'LL NEVER TAKE YOU FROM ME ANY MORE.

MINSTREL TRIO.

I'M A COMING – COMING – COMING,
AS THE ANGELS CLEAR THE WAY,
FAREWELL TO THE OLD KENTUCKY SHORE.

(Blackout. Sound of a large audience in an auditorium.)

*PROJECTION (4): POSTER
ANNOUNCING LINCOLN'S
APPEARANCE IN NEW YORK.*

THE ABOLITIONIST.

COME, ALL YE TRUE FRIENDS OF THE NATION...

(The others enter as supercilious **NEW YORKERS** *who have come to have a look at the Illinois rube. They speak directly to the audience, describing events as they unfold in front of them.)*

NEW YORKER 1 (LOVECRAFT). When Mr. Lincoln rose to speak, I was greatly disappointed.

NEW YORKER 2 (CASSIE). From his long, ungainly figure hung clothes that were evidently the work of an unskilled tailor.

NEW YORKER 3 (HAWK). His large feet, his clumsy hands, his bushy head, balanced on a long and lean head-stalk –

NEW YORKER 1. All this made a picture which did not fit in with New York's conception of a finished statesman.

THE ABOLITIONIST.

ATTEND TO HUMANITY'S CALL...

NEW YORKER 2. He cleared his throat and began.

NEW YORKER 4 (HANNIBAL). *(a high-pitched squawk)* "Mister *Cheer*-man!"

(All laugh discreetly except **NEW YORKER 5** *(***TRUD-GETT***), who has started to pay close attention.)*

NEW YORKER 1. He employed many other words with an old-fashioned pronunciation....

THE ABOLITIONIST.

COME AID IN THE SLAVE'S LIBERATION...

NEW YORKER 4. I said to myself, "You won't do."

NEW YORKER 1. This is all very well for the wild West...

NEW YORKER 3. …but it will never go down in New York!

THE ABOLITIONIST.
AND ROLL ON THE LIBERTY BALL!

THE ABOLITIONIST & NEW YORKER 5 (TRUDGETT).
AND ROLL ON THE LIBERTY BALL,
AND ROLL ON THE LIBERTY BALL,
COME AID IN THE SLAVE'S LIBERATION,
AND ROLL ON THE LIBERTY BALL!

NEW YORKER 4. But pretty soon he began to get into his subject….

NEW YORKER 2. He straightened up…

NEW YORKER 4. His face lighted as with an inward fire…

NEW YORKER 2. The whole man was transfigured.

THE ABOLITIONIST.
SUCCESS TO THE OLD-FASHIONED VIRTUE
THAT MEN ARE CREATED ALL FREE;
AND DOWN WITH THE POWER OF THE DESPOT,
WHEREVER HIS STRONGHOLD MAY BE!

THE ABOLITIONIST & NEW YORKERS 2, 4 & 5
WHEREVER HIS STRONGHOLD MAY BE,
WHEREVER HIS STRONGHOLD MAY BE;
AND DOWN WITH THE POWER OF THE DESPOT,
WHEREVER HIS STRONGHOLD MAY BE!

NEW YORKER 1. I forgot his peculiarities!

NEW YORKER 3. Presently, forgetting myself, I was on my feet with the rest…

NEW YORKER 1. yelling like a wild Indian…

NEW YORKER 3. cheering this wonderful man…

NEW YORKER 1. *(abandoning all restraint)* The greatest man since St. Paul!

PROJECTION (5): HEADLINE –
"THE PRAIRIES ON FIRE FOR LINCOLN!"

ALL.

HURRAH FOR THE CHOICE OF THE NATION,
OUR CHIEFTAIN SO BRAVE AND SO TRUE!
WE'LL GO FOR THE GREAT REFORMATION,
FOR LINCOLN AND LIBERTY, TOO!
WE'LL GO FOR THE SON OF KENTUCKY,
THE HERO OF HOOSIERDOM THROUGH,
THE PRIDE OF THE "SUCKERS" SO LUCKY,
FOR LINCOLN AND LIBERTY, TOO!

> *PROJECTION (6): HEADLINE –*
> *"LINCOLN NOMINATED!"*

THEN UP WITH THE BANNER SO GLORIOUS,
THE STAR-SPANGLED RED, WHITE AND BLUE!
WE'LL FIGHT 'TIL OUR BANNER'S VICTORIOUS –
FOR LINCOLN AND LIBERTY, TOO!

(Blackout. All exit except **HAWK.***)*

> *PROJECTION (7):*
> *"LET THE PEOPLE*
> *REJOICE! LINCOLN ELECTED!")*

*(***SECESSIONIST (HAWK)*** *steps into light.)*

SECESSIONIST (HAWK). *(ominously)* Even if the Potomac is crimsoned in human gore, the South will never submit to the inauguration of Abraham Lincoln.

(Projection out. Lights down on **HAWK.** **LOVE-CRAFT** *enters. With the addition of something as simple as a pair of glasses, he has become* **THE SEC-RETARY.***)*

THE SECRETARY (LOVECRAFT). I had just returned to Illinois from college in the East. My uncle practiced law next door to Mr. Lincoln and prevailed on his celebrated neighbor to offer me a secretarial post. When the great news of his election reached us, Mr. Lincoln turned to us. "Well, boys," he said, "your troubles are over. But mine have just begun."

PROJECTION (8): HEADLINE –
"THE UNION IS DISSOLVED!"

(**THE SECRETARY** *takes it in for a moment, then turns back to us, dismissing it.*)

He is convinced this is only an artificial crisis. More importantly, I am to accompany this backwoods Jupiter to Washington! At first he resisted – "We can't take all Illinois with us!" But then he smiled. "Well," he said, "let the young fellow come along."

(**A MAID (CASSIE)** *enters and helps* **THE SECRETARY** *into an overcoat. Sound of a train whistle.*)

After a farewell to his friends in Springfield, we boarded the eastbound train.

(**MAID** *exits, and he seats himself as though on a train next to the unseen Lincoln. He picks up a stack of mail and glances through it as he speaks.*)

All the talk now is of war. They say there's so much tension in Washington, a dogfight could make the gutters run with blood. The army insists Mr. Lincoln is in considerable danger.

(*A letter catches his eye – he opens it.*)

SECESSIONIST. Mr. Abe Lincoln: If you don't resign, we're going to put a spider in your dumpling, you god almighty goddamn son of a bitch! Excuse me for using such hard words with you, but you need it. (*politely*) Yours, etc.

(**THE SECRETARY** *looks up in alarm, but quickly recovers and puts the letter aside.*)

THE SECRETARY. Mr. Lincoln doesn't take these threats seriously – he says, "Oh, there's nothing like getting used to things."

(*He opens another.* **NORTHERN SPY (CORDELIA)** *enters furtively, checking to see she is not observed.*)

A NORTHERN SPY (CORDELIA). I was advised last night by a gentleman that there exists in Baltimore a league of ten persons who have sworn that you should never pass through that city alive.

(She slinks away. **THE SECRETARY** *rises, more concerned now.)*

THE SECRETARY. But a change in the traveling arrangements has brought us into Washington on the night train. There were no incidents, and for the next four years mail may be addressed to "A. Lincoln – The White House."

(Lights change as he crosses. He takes in the view, clearly unimpressed what he sees.)

So *this* is Washington. Springfield shines before me like a paradise compared with this miserable, sprawling little village which imagines itself a city.

(An elegantly dressed **FREEDWOMAN** *(CASSIE), comes through the door and is about to pass* **THE SECRETARY** *on her way out when he holds out his hat for her to take. This stops her.)*

THE FREEDWOMAN (CASSIE). *(not unkindly, indicating the door)* I believe you will find the servants through there.

(In some confusion at this unaccustomed response from a black woman, **THE SECRETARY** *exits through the door, hat still in hand.* **THE FREEDWOMAN** *turns back to the audience and continues, with great self-possession.)*

Mrs. Lincoln told several of her lady friends that she had an urgent need for a dressmaker. I was summoned. "We are just in from the West, and we are poor," she warned me. "I can't afford to pay big Eastern prices." *(with a smile)* I told her I thought there would be no difficulty about the charges.

(She starts off, but turns back.)

Mr. Lincoln is from the wilds of the West, and evil reports have said much of him and his wife. The polite world is shocked.

(Lights down. A crash of stage thunder and lightening.)

> *PROJECTION (9):*
> *"FORD'S ATHENEUM PRESENTS*
> *JAMES H. HACKETT'S COMPANY*
> *IN JULIUS CAESAR.")*

(MUSIC: "HAIL TO THE CHIEF." **HANNIBAL** *and* **TRUDGETT** *set a swag of bunting and arrange chairs to represent the President's box at the theatre.* **THE LADIES** *are seated upstage of the box.* **THE ACTOR (HAWK)** *strides Center, draped in a Roman toga.* **THE SECRETARY***, not pleased to be here, stands by an empty chair in the theatre box – this will be referred to throughout as if Lincoln were in it.)*

THE SECRETARY. *(confidentially, to us)* The Hell-Cat –

*(***THE WOMEN** *gasp and shoot him a disapproving look, and he catches himself.)*

– Mrs. Lincoln – has made it my task to accompany Mr. Lincoln to the theatre.

THE ACTOR (HAWK). *(declaiming ripely)*
"Either there is a civil strife in heaven,
Or else the world, too saucy with the gods,
Incenses them to send destruction."

(As the others applaud silently and **HAWK** *bows to them,* **THE SECRETARY** *nods toward the empty chair.)*

THE SECRETARY. *(uncomprehending)* Mr. Lincoln is fond of the theatre.

(THE ACTOR notices and hurls this right at THE SECRETARY.)

THE ACTOR.

"It is the part of men to fear and tremble
When the most mighty gods by tokens send
Such dreadful heralds to astonish us."

(A NEWSBOY (TRUDGETT) bursts in with a shout, carrying a stack of newspapers.)

NEWSBOY (TRUDGETT). Rebels fire on Fort Sumter!

(Pandemonium, as COMPANY rises and exits in all directions.)

THE SECRETARY. The newsboys came tearing and yelling up the street, even more furiously than usual.

NEWSBOY. Rebels take Fort Sumter!

> *PROJECTION (10):*
> *"75,000 MEN ORDERED OUT!"*

THE SECRETARY. The heather is on fire! The whole population seems to be in the streets with Union favors and flags. Even the White House is turned into a barracks! Everyone seems to be expecting a son or brother to arrive with the coming regiments.

NEWSBOY. *(front, with a grin)* If a fellow wants to go with a girl now – he'd better enlist!

(THE COMPANY re-enters as a small-town FARE-WELL COMMITTEE, headed by a pompous MAYOR (HAWK). Among them are THE FREEDWOMAN and THE FREEDMAN (HANNIBAL).)

ALL.

MAY GOD SAVE THE UNION,
GOD GRANT IT TO STAND;
THE PRIDE OF OUR PEOPLE,
THE BOAST OF OUR LAND.

STILL, STILL 'MID THE STORM
MAY OUR BANNER FLOAT FREE,
UNRENT AND UNRIVEN
O'ER EARTH AND O'ER SEA.

(During the song and hidden by the group, **TRUD-GETT** *dons a Union soldier's blouse, belt and cap. After the verse, he is revealed posing for a formal photograph in uniform.)*

*PROJECTION (11):
DAGUERROTYPE OF
TRUDGETT IN UNIFORM*

THE SOLDIER (TRUDGETT). We were presented with a flag by the ladies of the town. A young lady made a speech…

(A **HOMETOWN GIRL** *addresses the crowd, clutching a blue regimental flag to her bosom, perfectly thrilled at her own rhetoric.)*

HOMETOWN GIRL (CORDELIA). Sustain this banner for the love you bear to woman! For under no standard in the wide world is woman so blessed as are Columbia's daughters.

(But she has lost her place, and fumbles through her notes in a panic.)

THE SOLDIER. …but she went through with it about as smooth as one might come down a rocky hill in the dark.

HOMETOWN GIRL. *(recovering)* Our spirits waken and we feel the blood of heroes stirring in our veins!

(With a shiver of emotion, she builds to a big finish.)

The eagle of American liberty from her mountain eyrie swoops down on spreading pinions, and brave men rush to arms!

THE SOLDIER. The ladies then proposed three cheers for the colonel…

(As **THE LADIES** *delicately stab the air in silent cheers, there are 3 fiddle squawks from the pit.)*

…which sounded a good deal as my cat did when her tail was stepped on. The officers then gave the ladies three cheers…

*(***THE MEN** *throw their arms lustily into the air, accompanied by 3 warlike trumpet blasts.)*

…which made them turn pale.

*(***THE HOMETOWN GIRL** *swoons and starts blushingly from the stage. Realizing she is still holding the flag, she rushes back on, hands it to* **THE SOLDIER***, and runs off. Sound of a train whistle.)*

THE SOLDIER. *(with a shrug)* The band played, we took the flag…and went.

THE FREEDWOMAN. *(to* **THE FREEDMAN***)* A meeting of colored citizens was called to aid in the defense of the Union….

(Music stops.)

THE FREEDMAN (HANNIBAL). We were told by the police, "We want you damned niggers to keep out of this. This is a white man's war."

THE SOLDIER. *(making this sound perfectly reasonable)* I came out to fight for the Union – not to free the niggers.

*(***THE SOLDIER** *poses with* **THE MAYOR** *for an unseen photographer.* **THE FREEDWOMAN** *looks back at* **THE FREEDMAN** *with concern.)*

THE SOLDIER, THE FREEDWOMAN, HAWK & LOVECRAFT.
MAY GOD SAVE THE UNION,
THE RED, WHITE AND BLUE;
OUR STATES KEEP UNITED
THE DREARY DAY THROUGH;
LET THE STARS TELL THE TALE
OF OUR GLORIOUS PAST
AND BIND US IN UNION
FOREVER TO LAST.

(Lights out on **THE FAREWELL COMMITTEE***, isolating* **THE FREEDMAN***.)*

THE FREEDMAN. Our national sin has found us out. The war now being waged is a war for and against slavery – it can never be put down till one or the other of these vital forces is completely destroyed. Would to God you would let us do something! We lack nothing but your consent.

(Blackout. **THE FREEDMAN** *exits.)*

> *PROJECTION (12): TITLE CARD –*
> *"MISS HOPEWELL IN 'ABRAHAM'S*
> *DAUGHTER – THE SONG OF THE*
> *FIRE ZOUAVES.'"*

(Footlights up on a **MUSIC HALL SINGER (CORDELIA)** *dressed in a flattering theatrical version of an exotic Zouave uniform. She holds a rifle high above her head.)*

MUSIC HALL SINGER (CORDELIA).
OH! KIND FOLKS LISTEN TO MY SONG,
IT IS NO IDLE STORY,
IT'S ALL ABOUT A VOLUNTEER
WHO'S GOIN' TO FIGHT FOR GLORY!
NOW DON'T YOU THINK THAT I AM RIGHT?
FOR I AM NOTHING SHORTER!
AND I BELONG TO THE FIRE ZOUAVES,
AND DON'T YOU THINK I OUGHTER?
I'M GOIN' DOWN TO WASHINGTON
TO FIGHT FOR ABRAHAM'S DAUGHTER!

*(***MUSIC HALL ENTERTAINERS (LOVECRAFT & HAWK)***, wearing Zouave caps and jackets, join her in a flashy show-biz parody of a precision rifle drill.)*

MUSIC HALL SINGER.
OH! SHOULD YOU ASK ME WHO SHE AM,
COLUMBIA IS HER NAME, SIR!

MUSIC HALL SINGER. *(cont.)*

> SHE IS THE CHILD OF ABRAHAM
> OR UNCLE SAM – THE SAME, SIR!
> NOW IF I FIGHT, WHY AIN'T I RIGHT?
> AND DON'T YOU THINK I OUGHTER?
> THE VOLUNTEERS ARE POURING IN
> FROM EVERY LOYAL QUARTER –
> I'M GOIN' DOWN TO WASHINGTON
> TO FIGHT FOR ABRAHAM'S DAUGHTER!

(Music under the following. **THE FREEDMAN &**
THE SOLDIER *enter.)*

THE FREEDMAN. Each man has been provided with a piece of rope with which to bring back a prisoner from the audacious South, to be led in a noose, on their early and triumphant return.

THE SOLDIER. Our regiment yells at everything. A yell starts in at one end of the division, and regiment after regiment takes it up and carries it along, then sends it back to the other end – few knowing what it was about, and caring less.

> *PROJECTION (13):*
> *"ON TO RICHMOND!"*

THE FREEDMAN. Our brave army moves toward Manassas, and thence without delay – to Richmond!

MUSIC HALL SINGER.

> BUT LET US LAY ALL JOKES ASIDE,
> IT IS A SORRY QUESTION –
> THE MAN WHO WOULD THESE STATES DIVIDE
> SHOULD HANG FOR HIS SUGGESTION!
> ONE COUNTRY AND ONE FLAG, I SAY,
> WHOE'ER THE WAR MAY SLAUGHTER!
> SO I'M GOIN' AS A FIRE ZOUAVE,
> AND DON'T YOU THINK I OUGHTER?
> I'M GOIN' DOWN TO WASHINGTON –

ALL. *(a shout)*

> TO FIGHT FOR ABRAHAM'S DAUGHTER!

(They freeze in a triumphant tableau. They remain a moment in the light, before **THE FREEDWOMAN** *appears.)*

THE FREEDWOMAN.
'MID PLEASURES AND PALACES,
THOUGH WE MAY ROAM,
BE IT EVER SO HUMBLE,
THERE'S NO PLACE LIKE HOME....

(Music continues under, as the tableau disintegrates.)

THE FREEDWOMAN. The road to Manassas was choked with Sunday picnickers rushing off to see their loyal heroes teach the rebels a lesson. The rest of us waited for news of the victory. But the defeated Union troops commenced pouring into Washington at daylight on Monday. A steady stream of men, covered with mud, poured up Pennsylvania Avenue.

*(***THE FREEDMAN*** opens the window and calls out toward stage in alarm.)*

THE FREEDMAN. Where are you all coming from?

THE SOLDIER. *(angry and humiliated)* I guess we're all coming out of Virginny as far as we can – and pretty well whipped, too.

THE FREEDMAN. *(can't believe it)* What! The whole army?

THE SOLDIER. They can stay that like. I know I'm going home. I've had enough fighting to last my lifetime.

*(***THE SOLDIER*** exits.)*

PROJECTION (14):
SELF-SATISFIED OFFICERS
IN FULL DRESS UNIFORMS.

THE FREEDWOMAN. *(scornfully)* The bar at Willard's Hotel is full of officers. There you are, shoulder straps! But where are your men?

THE FREEDMAN. Bull Run is your work. Had you been one-tenth worthy of your men, this never would have happened.

THE SECRETARY. Well. The fat's in the fire now. And we shall have to crow very small until we can retrieve the disgrace somehow.

(Lights down, all exit.)

> *PROJECTION (15):*
> *"PRESIDENT CALLS FOR*
> *500,000 VOLUNTEERS."*

(Wearing a traveling cloak, **THE NURSE (CORDE-LIA)** *enters. She is a no-nonsense New Englander who has heard quite enough defeatist talk. Throughout the following she packs a valise.)*

THE NURSE (CORDELIA). It is not characteristic of Americans to sit down despondently after a defeat. Let us go to work, then, with a will. A townswoman heard of my desire to become a nurse and brought about an interview with one of the sisterhood which I wished to join. A morning chat produced three results: I felt that I could do the work, was offered a place, and accepted it – promising not to desert, but to stand ready to march on Washington.

(She picks up a small photo case and places it in the grip before snapping it shut and crossing purposefully away. Sound of a train whistle, and the light change.)

It was dark when we arrived. Though I'd often been told that Washington was a spacious place, its visible magnitude quite took my breath away. The White House was lighted up, and carriages were rolling in and out of the great gate. I would have liked a peep through the crack of the door.

*(***A SENTRY (TRUDGETT)*** leans casually against the office door, rifle at his side.)*

We stopped before a great pile of buildings, with a flag flying before it, sentinels at the door, and a very trying quantity of men lounging about. My heart beat rather faster than usual, and it suddenly struck me that I was very far from home.

(She takes a deep breath. As she approaches the door, **THE SENTRY** *stands at attention, touches his cap and opens the door for her.)*

THE NURSE. *(cont.)* Marching boldly up the steps, the men fell back, the guard touched their caps, a boy opened the door, and, as it closed behind me, I felt that my mission was begun.

(Lights down as she exits through the door. Lights up on theatre box as before. MUSIC: HAIL TO THE CHIEF.)

> *PROJECTION (16):*
> *"FORD'S ATHENEUM PRESENTS*
> *JAMES H. HACKETT'S COMPANY IN*
> *HENRY IV, PART 1."*

*(***THE SECRETARY*** is standing behind Lincoln's chair, in a sour mood.)*

THE SECRETARY. The Hell-cat gets more hell-cattical every day. Her Satanic Majesty has now decreed that it shall be my duty to protect the President's dignity in public. We come to the theatre with alarming frequency – it's about the only place he can escape to. The cowardly shame of Bull Run has created a sea of troubles.

(Music: Fanfare. **THE ACTOR (HAWK)** *enters swinging a broadsword melodramatically at an unseen foe, thrilling all except* **THE SECRETARY**.*)*

How funny that he should be so completely absorbed in these human jackstraws, moving about with their silly little gestures and

THE SECRETARY. *(cont.)* flatulent text. Not much different from our generals. If only we had one who could do more than talk!

(A PORTER *(*HANNIBAL*) bursts in and hands a telegram to* THE SECRETARY.*)*

PORTER (HANNIBAL). For the President!

(As THE SECRETARY *looks over the telegram,* THE PORTER *speaks the words.)*

"Secession is killed in Western Virginia. General George B. McClellan."

(Music: "The Marseillaise.")

> PROJECTION (17):
> GENERAL GEORGE McCLELLAN,
> POSED LIKE NAPOLEON.

*(*THE ACTOR, *striking a pretty heroic pose himself, speaks as Henry IV.)*

THE ACTOR (HAWK). "Thus ever did rebellion find rebuke!"

THE SECRETARY. *(enthusiastically dictating a telegram)* "From the President. General McClellan: Circumstances make your presence here necessary. Come hither without delay."

(Drumroll, which will be used throughout to accompany the frequent changes in Union command, as HANNIBAL *reveals an intimidating portrait of General* MCCLELLAN *above the set.)*

THE ACTOR.

"Rebellion in this land shall lose his sway,
Meeting the check of such another day!"

(During the next song, HANNIBAL *helps* HAWK *exchange his crown and doublet for the gold-bedecked uniform coat of a Union Major General,*

assuming the role of **MCCLELLAN**. *This should take place in full view of the audience and call to mind a matador being dressed in his "suit of lights." Finally,* **HANNIBAL** *places the cap on his head like a crown.)*

THE FREEDWOMAN.
THE ARMY IS GATHERING
FROM NEAR AND FROM FAR –
THE TRUMPET IS SOUNDING
THE CALL FOR THE WAR!

THE SOLDIER.
MCCLELLAN'S OUR LEADER,
HE'S GALLANT AND STRONG!
WE'LL GIRD ON THE ARMOR
AND BE MARCHING ALONG.

ALL.
MARCHING ALONG,
WE ARE MARCHING ALONG!
GIRD ON THE ARMOR
AND BE MARCHING ALONG!
MCCLELLAN'S OUR LEADER,
HE'S GALLANT AND STRONG –
FOR GOD AND FOR COUNTRY
WE ARE MARCHING ALONG!

(HAWK*'s transition to the narcissistic* **MCCLELLAN** *is complete.)*

MCCLELLAN (HAWK).
THE FOE IS BEFORE US
IN BATTLE ARRAY –
BUT LET US NOT WAVER
OR TURN FROM THE WAY!
THE LORD IS OUR STRENGTH
AND THE UNION'S OUR SONG!
WITH COURAGE AND FAITH
WE ARE MARCHING ALONG.

ALL.

> MARCHING ALONG,
> WE ARE MARCHING ALONG!
> GIRD ON THE ARMOR
> AND BE MARCHING ALONG!
> OUR CAUSE IS THE RIGHT ONE –
> OUR FOE'S IN THE WRONG!
> THEN GLADLY WE'LL SING
> AS WE'RE MARCHING ALONG.

> *(Music continues under.)*

MCCLELLAN. When I see the hand of God guarding one so weak as myself, I almost think myself a chosen instrument.

THE SECRETARY. "From the President. General McClellan: You have been designated to command all our armies. This command will entail a vast labor upon you."

> *(All turn to* **MCCLELLAN**.*)*

MCCLELLAN. *(sincerely, reassuringly)* I can do it all.

> *(A cheer from* **THE COMPANY**.*)*

> THE FLAG OF OUR COUNTRY
> IS FLOATING ON HIGH –
> WE'LL STAND BY THAT FLAG
> TILL WE CONQUER OR DIE!

ALL BUT MCCLELLAN.

> MCCLELLAN'S OUR LEADER,
> HE'S GALLANT AND STRONG –

ADD MCCLELLAN.

> FOR GOD AND FOR COUNTRY
> WE ARE MARCHING ALONG!

> *(Music continues under, as* **MCCLELLAN** *composes a letter to his unseen wife.)*

MCCLELLAN. My Dearest Ellen: I find myself in a new and strange position here – by some strange operation of magic I seem to have become the power of the land. I receive letter after letter alluding to the Presidency, Dictatorship, etc. But as I hope one day to be united with you forever in heaven, I have no such aspirations – I will never accept the Presidency. Pray for me, darling, that I may be able to accomplish my task – the greatest, perhaps, that any poor, weak mortal ever had to do.

ALL BUT MCCLELLAN.
MCCLELLAN'S OUR LEADER,
HE'S GALLANT AND STRONG –

ADD MCCLELLAN.
FOR GOD AND FOR COUNTRY
WE ARE MARCHING ALONG!

(**MCCLELLAN** *twirls his cap overhead, accepting the adulation of his unseen troops.*)

ALL.
MARCHING ALONG,
WE ARE MARCHING ALONG!
GIRD ON THE ARMOR
AND BE MARCHING ALONG!
MCCLELLAN'S OUR LEADER,
HE'S GALLANT AND STRONG –
FOR GOD AND FOR COUNTRY
WE ARE MARCHING ALONG!

PROJECTION (18):
THE HALF-BUILT
CAPITOL DOME.

(*A canvas drape is lowered to resemble a field tent over the entrance downstage left, opposite Lincoln's office.* **MCCLELLAN** *and* **THE SECRETARY** *take up positions accordingly.*)

MCCLELLAN. To the War Department: All quiet along the Potomac.

THE SECRETARY. *(who loves to gossip)* I call Mr. Lincoln "the Tycoon." And he might as well be the Grand Tycoon of Japan, he rules my life so completely. Last night at midnight, he burst into my room in his slippers, as he wanted to read me a funny poem. The Tycoon seemed utterly unconscious that with his nightshirt hanging above his long legs and setting out behind like the tail feathers of an enormous ostrich, he was infinitely funnier than anything in his book.

MCCLELLAN. I had dinner with the President last night. What a rare bird he is! I never in my life met anyone so full of anecdote.

THE SECRETARY. Underneath his stories from third-class county barrooms, the Tycoon keeps a fountain of first-class practical wisdom.

MCCLELLAN. His stories were as usual very pertinent – and some pretty good!

(Two fluttery **WASHINGTON LADIES (CORDELIA & CASSIE)** *join him.* **MCCLELLAN** *mimes the action described below.)*

THE SECRETARY. *(not without envy)* As for "The Young Napoleon," every hostess in the capital has the general in her sights, and why not? He's the very model of chivalry – and about as modest as one could be who is so universally adored. The General does a nice piece of after-dinner claptrap – he bends a ten-dollar gold piece right in half between his finger and his thumb.

*(***THE LADIES*** *nearly swoon with admiration.* **THE SECRETARY** *takes this in, then continues dryly.)*

The ladies are always impressed.

MCCLELLAN. *(pleased with himself)* "To the War Department: All quiet along the Potomac."

(MUSIC under: "COMRADES, FILL NO GLASS FOR ME.")

> *PROJECTION (19):*
> *UNION TROOPS DRILLING.*

*(**THE SOLDIER** drags in, lugging a rifle. He tosses his knapsack on the ground with relief.)*

THE SOLDIER. *(disgusted)* The first thing in the morning is drill, then drill, then drill again. Then drill, drill, a little more drill. Then drill, and lastly, drill. Between drills, we drill.

MCCLELLAN. I have found no army to command – merely a collection of regiments cowering on the banks of the Potomac. The troops are demoralized by the defeat at Bull Run – some regiments even mutinous.

THE SOLDIER. *(sprawled on the ground)* If there is anything peculiarly attractive in marching 20 miles a day under a scorching sun with a good mule load, my mind is not of a sufficiently poetical nature to appreciate it.

*(**THE SOLDIER** produces a jug. To his indescribable disappointment, it is empty.)*

> *PROJECTION (20):*
> *A JOYLESS PHOTO*
> *OF THE U.S. CHRISTIAN*
> *COMMISSION.*

*(**A TEMPERANCE LADY (CORDELIA)** enters, an energetic Victorian do-gooder. Outraged at the sight of the Soldier's jug, she pounces on **MCCLELLAN**.)*

TEMPERANCE LADY (CORDELIA). There is at present the most serious apprehension that the Grand Army of the Potomac is on the eve of a terrible defeat. Not from the rebels, but from rum!

MCCLELLAN. *(trying to placate her)* It has come to my attention that the men are frequenting... *(he reaches for a polite word)* ...disorderly houses.

TEMPERANCE LADY. Thousands on thousands of young men not yet inured to tipple are now induced to swallow their daily glass.

MCCLELLAN. No one evil agent so much obstructs this army as the degrading vice of drunkenness. It is therefore ordered that the Provost Guard shall arrest any man found at the following establishments: Madam Wilton's Private Residence for Ladies, the Blue Goose... and Madam Russell's Bake Oven.

THE SOLDIER. The Colonel's drunk all the time now. He turned out fifteen gallons of rotgut and several of the boys got happy. Some got pugilistic.

MCCLELLAN. *(at his wit's end)* I have come to the belief that total abstinence from intoxicating liquors would be worth 50,000 men to this army!

*(**MCCLELLAN** and **TEMPERANCE LADY** cross to **THE SOLDIER**.)*

MCCLELLAN.

OH, COMRADES, FILL NO GLASS FOR ME
TO DROWN MY SOUL IN LIQUID FLAME!

MCCLELLAN & TEMPERANCE LADY.

FOR IF I DRANK, THE TOAST SHOULD BE
TO BLIGHTED FORTUNE, HEALTH AND FAME.

TEMPERANCE LADY.

YET THOUGH I LONG TO QUELL THE STRIFE
THAT PASSION HOLDS AGAINST MY LIFE,

MCCLELLAN.

STILL, BOON COMPANIONS YE MAY BE –
BUT COMRADES, FILL NO GLASS FOR ME.

(The others have entered, and now join in.)

ALL.

STILL, BOON COMPANIONS YE MAY BE,
BUT COMRADES, FILL NO GLASS FOR ME.

(Music continues under.)

THE SOLDIER. *(ashamed)* Last night I had plenty of whiskey but today I have none.

(Shame and pride in his exploits battle for the upper hand.)

We had five canteens full. We had a merry old time and tore everything upside down. I thought I would fire a salute, so I got my musket and fired it – and I set my tent on fire. By the time I got through, my tent was burnt up.

TEMPERANCE LADY. *(consoling him)* You poor boy.

(to the others)

This is what comes of yielding to the demon!

*(to **THE SOLDIER**)*

A temperance league has been formed, and a goodly number of men stand pledges to wholly abstain from the use of intoxicating drinks.

*(Whether driven by commitment to an improved lifestyle or proximity to a lovely young woman, **THE SOLDIER** launches his hand into the air to take the pledge.)*

THE SOLDIER.

THEN, BY A MOTHER'S SACRED TEAR,
BY ALL THAT MEMORY SHOULD REVERE,
THOUGH BOON COMPANIONS YE MAY BE –
OH! COMRADES, FILL NO GLASS FOR ME!

ALL.

THOUGH BOON COMPANIONS YE MAY BE...

*(**A SALOONKEEPER (HANNIBAL)** reveals a sign upstage reading "MADAME DUPREZ'S CLUB*

*HOUSE: RELAXATION FOR GENTLEMEN". He
beckons* **THE SOLDIER***, who hesitates for a moment,
then turns front with a shrug.)*

THE SOLDIER. Oh, well. A birthday don't come but
once a year. And tents are cheap!

*(He scurries off through the doorway, unnoticed by
the others.)*

ALL.

OH! COMRADES, FILL NO GLASS FOR ME!

(As **MCCLELLAN** *and* **THE TEMPERANCE LADY**
*finally notice their quarry has escaped, the lights
bump out.)*

> *PROJECTION (21):
> "GENERAL MCCLELLAN SAYS
> TROOPS ARE READY."*

THE FREEDWOMAN. The First Lady says General McClellan is a humbug. He talks so much – and does so
little.

MCCLELLAN. My Dearest Ellen: You have no idea how
the men brighten up now when I go among them.
I can see every eye glisten. If you could witness the
enthusiasm of the troops, their confidence and
desire to meet the enemy – I am sure that you
would agree with me in feeling confident of success.

THE SECRETARY. He says his troops are ready, but the
impression is daily gaining ground that The Young
Napoleon does not intend to do anything.

MCCLELLAN. *(turning to* **THE SECRETARY***)* I shall
crush the rebels in one campaign! To the War
Department –

THE SECRETARY. *(disgusted, finishing for him)* "All quiet
along the Potomac."

(They exit. Lights up on **THE NURSE**, *seated in the window above stage. As she sings,* **SENTRY (TRUD-GETT)** *enters in half-light.)*

THE NURSE.

"ALL QUIET ALONG THE POTOMAC" TONIGHT,
WHERE THE SOLDIERS LIE PEACEFULLY DREAMING,
AND THEIR TENTS IN THE RAYS OF THE CLEAR
    AUTUMN MOON,
AND THE LIGHT OF THE CAMPFIRES ARE GLEAMING.
A TREMULOUS SIGH, AS THE GENTLE NIGHT WIND
THROUGH THE FOREST LEAVES SLOWLY IS CREEPING –
WHILE THE STARS UP ABOVE, WITH THEIR GLITTERING
    EYES,
KEEP GUARD O'ER THE ARMY WHILE SLEEPING.

MCCLELLAN.

"ALL QUIET ALONG THE POTOMAC TONIGHT."

THE NURSE.

"ALL QUIET ALONG THE POTOMAC" TONIGHT –
EXCEPT HERE AND THERE A STRAY PICKET
IS SHOT AS HE WALKS ON HIS BEAT TO AND FRO,
BY A RIFLEMAN HID IN THE THICKET.
'TIS NOTHING – A PRIVATE OR TWO NOW AND THEN
WILL NOT COUNT IN THE NEWS OF THE BATTLE:
NOT AN OFFICER LOST, ONLY ONE OF THE MEN
MOANING OUT ALL ALONE THE DEATH RATTLE.

MCCLELLAN.

"ALL QUIET ALONG THE POTOMAC TONIGHT."

THE NURSE.

HARK! WAS IT THE NIGHT WIND THAT RUSTLED THE
    LEAVES?
WAS IT MOONLIGHT SO WONDROUSLY FLASHING?
IT LOOKED LIKE A RIFLE –

*(***THE SENTRY*** jerks backward as though shot, crumpling to the floor as he reaches out toward us.)*

SENTRY (TRUDGETT).

AH! MARY, GOOD-BYE!

THE NURSE.

AND HIS LIFEBLOOD IS EBBING AND PLASHING!
"ALL QUIET ALONG THE POTOMAC TONIGHT" –
NO SOUND SAVE THE RUSH OF THE RIVER!
WHILE SOFT FALLS THE DEW ON THE FACE OF THE
    DEAD –

(spoken)

The picket's off duty forever.

(sung)

"ALL QUIET ALONG THE POTOMAC TONIGHT."

(Lights to black. Lights up on **THE FREEDMAN**
Center, a smug **MCCLELLAN** *at his tent downstage
left, and a very agitated* **SECRETARY** *by the office
door downstage right.)*

THE SECRETARY. The Tycoon keeps poking sharp sticks
under McClellan's ribs, but he doesn't move.

MCCLELLAN. Dearest Ellen: I have restored order completely. I have Washington perfectly quiet now
– you wouldn't know there was a regiment here.

THE FREEDMAN. Yesterday the army was reviewed by
President Lincoln and General McClellan.

*(***THE SOLDIER*** enters, as* **THE SECRETARY** *and*
MCCLELLAN *circle the playing area, reviewing the
troops.* **THE SOLDIER** *stands at attention facing
upstage, turning to speak to us over his shoulder.)*

THE SOLDIER. Today the colonel gave us the honor of
tagging behind old "Honest Abe" himself. I got a
look at him up close. And I can tell you that any
man that homely *ought* to be honest.

THE FREEDMAN. The soldiers received General McClellan with loud shouts. They believed in him. And
so did I. *(ironically)* And had I stood in the ranks, I
should have shouted with the lustiest of them.

(He exits.)

MCCLELLAN. They nearly pulled me to pieces in one regiment. You never heard such yelling.

(He smiles.)

I do not think the President liked it much.

THE SECRETARY. *(making sure the general hears this)* The Tycoon calls him an admirable engineer, but says his talent is for a stationary engine.

MCCLELLAN. *(hotly)* There are some of the greatest geese in this administration I have ever seen. Even the President supposes himself capable of conducting great military operations!

THE SECRETARY. *(the last straw)* This army has got to fight or run away. The champagne and oysters on the Potomac must be stopped!

*(***THE SECRETARY & MCCLELLAN*** move angrily toward each other. ***THE SOLDIER*** steps between them and sings. Staging has the feel of a minstrel show number, minus the dialect.)*

THE SOLDIER.
WAY DOWN IN OLD VIRGINNY,
I SUPPOSE YOU ALL DO KNOW,
THEY HAVE TRIED TO BUST THE UNION, BUT THEY
    FIND IT IS NO GO!

MCCLELLAN.
THE YANKEE BOYS ARE STARTING OUT THE UNION
    FOR TO SAVE,

THE SOLDIER & MCCLELLAN.
AND WE'RE MARCHING DOWN TO WASHINGTON…

THE SECRETARY. *(interrupting)*
TO FIGHT FOR UNCLE ABE!

ALL THREE.
RIP, RAP, FLIP, FLAP,
STRAP YOUR KNAPSACK ON YOUR BACK!
FOR WE'RE A-GOIN' TO WASHINGTON
TO FIGHT FOR UNCLE ABE!

(Music continues under. The tension between **MCCLELLAN** *and* **THE SECRETARY** *builds throughout the number.)*

MCCLELLAN. If they will simply let me alone, I feel confident of success. The salvation of the country demands the utmost prudence on my part. This war should be conducted upon the highest principles known to Christian civilization. And we must stay clear of the Negro question at all costs.

ALL 3.

RIP, RAP, FLIP, FLAP,
STRAP YOUR KNAPSACK ON YOUR BACK!
FOR WE'RE A-GOIN' TO WASHINGTON
TO FIGHT FOR UNCLE ABE!

THE SECRETARY. *(seething)* Last evening, the Tycoon went over to General McClellan's house. After an hour, McClellan came in, and the servant told him the President was waiting to see him. We waited another half-an-hour and sent the servant once more to tell the General we were there. The answer coolly came that the General had gone to bed. *(mystified)* But the Tycoon says, "I'll hold McClellan's horse if he'll only bring us success."

ALL 3.

RIP, RAP, FLIP, FLAP,
STRAP YOUR KNAPSACK ON YOUR BACK!
FOR WE'RE A-GOIN' TO WASHINGTON
TO FIGHT FOR UNCLE ABE!

MCCLELLAN. *(sarcastically)* I saw the President again, and was of course much edified by his anecdotes – ever apropos, and ever unworthy of one holding his high position. He is nothing more than a well-meaning baboon.

THE SECRETARY. *(a Lincolnesque twang)* "If McClellan isn't using the Army, I'd like to borrow it for a while."

MCCLELLAN. *(reacting to the implied threat)* The rascals are after me again! And so, my dearest Ellen, I shall leave here on the wing for Richmond – which you may be sure I will take!

> *PROJECTION (22):*
> *A SEA OF ARTILLERY*
> *ON THE MOVE.*

THE SECRETARY. *(hugely relieved)* McClellan is at last in motion and is moving on Richmond.

THE SOLDIER.

> THE SEASON NOW IS COMING WHEN THE ROADS
>   BEGIN TO DRY –
> SOON THE ARMY OF THE POTOMAC WILL MAKE THE
>   REBELS FLY!
> FOR MCCLELLAN, HE'S THE MAN, THE UNION FOR TO
>   SAVE!
> OH! "HAIL COLUMBIA'S" RIGHT SIDE UP, AND SO'S
>   YOUR UNCLE ABE!

ALL 3.

> RIP, RAP, FLIP, FLAP,
> STRAP YOUR KNAPSACK ON YOUR BACK!
> FOR WE'RE A-GOIN' TO WASHINGTON
> TO FIGHT FOR UNCLE ABE!

MCCLELLAN. *(with urgency)* To the President: If I am not reinforced, it is probable that I will be obliged to fight nearly double my numbers.

THE SECRETARY. *(exasperated again)* Now The Young Napoleon sits trembling at Yorktown, afraid either to fight or run.

MCCLELLAN. I must have more troops!

THE SECRETARY. From the President: "You now have over a hundred thousand troops. It is indispensable to you that you strike a blow. I am powerless to help you in this."

MCCLELLAN. Those hounds in Washington are after me again. I must have more troops!

THE SECRETARY. Even if the Tycoon could by some magic send a hundred thousand men, McClellan would suddenly discover that the rebels have four hundred thousand.

(He tries to stay calm.)

THE SECRETARY. *(cont.)* From the President: "I have never written to you in greater kindness of feeling than now. But you must act!"

*(Forced at last to action, **MCCLELLAN** strides upstage to address his unseen army, letting out all the rhetorical stops.)*

MCCLELLAN. Soldiers of the Army of the Potomac! I will bring you now face to face with the rebels. You know that your General loves you from the depths of his heart. And when this sad war is over, we will all return to our homes, to ask no higher honor than the proud consciousness that we belonged to the Army of the Potomac!

(Music now at a deliberate cakewalk tempo.)

ALL 3.

RIP, RAP, FLIP, FLAP,
STRAP YOUR KNAPSACK ON YOUR BACK!
FOR WE'RE A-GOIN' TO WASHINGTON
TO FIGHT,
TO FIGHT,
TO FIGHT....

> *PROJECTION (23):*
> *"ON TO RICHMOND!"*

RIP, RAP, FLIP, FLAP,
STRAP YOUR KNAPSACK ON YOUR BACK!
FOR WE'RE A-GOIN' TO WASHINGTON
TO FIGHT FOR UNCLE ABE!

(Blackout. Sound: all hell breaks loose – bugle calls, cannon, the works. 3 projections in rapid succession:)

PROJECTIONS (24, 25, 26):
TROOPS IN COMBAT.

(Lights up on **CASSIE**, **CORDELIA**, **LOVECRAFT &**
HANNIBAL *as an upbeat group of Union support-*
ers.)

SINGERS.
HURRAH! HURRAH! HURRAH!
SOUND THE NEWS FROM THE DIN OF BATTLE
    BOOMING!
TELL THE PEOPLE FAR AND WIDE
THAT BETTER TIMES ARE COMING!

(Music: a flatulent bugle call, and **THE SOLDIER**
slumps in, rifle dragging behind him.)

THE SOLDIER. Either we've just made an inglorious ske-
daddle – or one brilliant retreat.

*(***MCCLELLAN** *enters from his tent.)*

MCCLELLAN. *(coming positively unglued)* We have –

(He can't bring himself to say the word.)

– *failed to win* – only because overpowered by supe-
rior numbers. I have lost this battle because my
force was too small.

THE SECRETARY. *(amazed at his cluelessness)* Since Don
Quixote's enumeration of the armies of King Pen-
tapolin of the Naked Arm, there has been nothing
like our General's vision of the Rebel forces.

MCCLELLAN. I repeat that I am not responsible for this.
And I say it with the earnestness of a General who
feels in his heart the loss of every brave man who
has been needlessly sacrificed.

THE SECRETARY. *(finally)* From the President. "General:
You are ordered to withdraw your army."

MCCLELLAN. *(judgment deserting him completely)* If I save
this army now, I tell you plainly that I owe no
thanks to you or any other persons in Washington.
You have done your best to sacrifice this army!

(A beat. Then:)

MACCLELLAN. *(cont.)* Send more gunboats.

*(**HANNIBAL** crosses to **MCCLELLAN**'s portrait.)*

THE SECRETARY. General Pope will assume command.

*(Drumroll. **HANNIBAL** tugs on the rope. **MCCLEL-LAN**'s portrait is replaced by a smug portrait of General John Pope, as **MCCLELLAN** walks upstage in defeat. **THE SINGERS** start again hopefully.)*

SINGERS.

HURRAH! HURRAH! HURRAH!

*(**HANNIBAL** hands a telegram to **THE SECRETARY**.)*

HANNIBAL. From General Pope. "I come to you out of the West, where we have always seen the backs of our enemies. My headquarters will be in the saddle."

(Music: another flatulent bugle.)

> PROJECTION (26.1):
> "POPE'S ARMY ROUTED."

*(Disgusted, **THE SOLDIER** jerks a thumb toward Pope's portrait.)*

THE SOLDIER. Looks like his headquarters were where his hindquarters should have been.

*(The dejected **SINGERS** lower their heads and slink back across stage.)*

THE SECRETARY. *(facing the inevitable)* Well, we're whipped again. McClellan has the army with him, and the Tycoon says we must use what tools we have. If McClellan can't fight himself, he excels in making others ready to fight.

*(Drumroll. **HANNIBAL** pulls the rope to restore **MCCLELLAN**'s portrait. Music: "The Marseillaise." **MCCLELLAN** crosses slowly straight downstage, waving his cap overhead triumphantly.)*

THE SOLDIER. *(a shout of joy)* Little Mac is back!

(MUSIC under: "MARCHING ALONG".)

> *PROJECTION (27):*
> *A HEROIC MCCLELLAN PASSING*
> *ON HORSEBACK THROUGH*
> *AN ADORING CROWD.*

MCCLELLAN. *(attempting humility)* I leave to others who were present the description...

THE SOLDIER. We threw our caps high into the air, and danced and frolicked like school-boys.

MCCLELLAN. *(but failing)* ...the frantic cheers of welcome that extended for miles...

THE SOLDIER. We cheered and cheered again, till we became so hoarse we could cheer no longer.

MCCLELLAN. ...the wild appeals of the men that I should take them back and snatch victory out of defeat!

THE SOLDIER. Hundreds of us hugged his horse's legs while the general pointed with his finger to the mountain.

(MCCLELLAN duplicates this pose. Awed by his magnificence, THE SOLDIER drinks it in.)

It was like a great scene in a play.

MCCLELLAN. Dearest Ellen: Again I have been called upon to save the country. The case is desperate, but with God's help I will try unselfishly to do my best and, if he wills it, accomplish the salvation of the nation.

(MCCLELLAN starts to exit, then turns back.)

But I must have more troops.

(He exits. Blackout. THE GUIDE enters.)

THE GUIDE (CASSIE). They may send the flower of their young men to die. They may send them one year, two years, three years – till they tire of sending, or till they use up the young men. All of no use. God is ahead of Mr. Lincoln.

(She exits.)

> *PROJECTION (28):*
> *"PRESIDENT CALLS FOR*
> *300,000 VOLUNTEERS."*

(Llights up on **THE NURSE.***)*

THE NURSE.

WE ARE COMING, FATHER ABR'AM,
THREE HUNDRED THOUSAND MORE –
FROM MISSISSIPPI'S WINDING STREAM
AND FROM NEW ENGLAND'S SHORE.

*(***THE SOLDIER** *enters.)*

THE SOLDIER

WE LEAVE OUR PLOWS AND WORKSHOPS,
OUR WIVES AND CHILDREN DEAR,
WITH HEARTS TOO FULL FOR UTTERANCE,
WITH BUT A SILENT TEAR.

*(***THE SECRETARY** *enters.)*

THE SECRETARY.

WE DARE NOT LOOK BEHIND US,
BUT STEADFASTLY BEFORE.
WE ARE COMING, FATHER ABR'AM,
THREE HUNDRED THOUSAND MORE!

ALL.

WE ARE COMING, WE ARE COMING,
OUR UNION TO RESTORE!
WE ARE COMING, FATHER ABR'AM,
WITH THREE HUNDRED THOUSAND MORE.
WE ARE COMING, FATHER ABR'AM,
WITH THREE HUNDRED THOUSAND MORE.

(Music continues under.)

THE SOLDIER. I gave up my job at John D. Pringle's, for I did not feel I was doing my duty to stay at home when nearly all my comrades was leaving for the seat of war. I was sworn into the U.S. Service, put on the Army blue for the first time, and feel first rate!

THE SOLDIER.
IF YOU LOOK UP ALL OUR VALLEYS
WHERE THE GROWING HARVESTS SHINE,
YOU MAY SEE OUR STURDY FARMER BOYS
FAST FORMING INTO LINE;
AND CHILDREN FROM THEIR MOTHER'S KNEES
ARE PULLING AT THE WEEDS,
AND LEARNING HOW TO REAP AND SOW
AGAINST THEIR COUNTRY'S NEEDS.

THE SOLDIER & THE NURSE.
AND A FAREWELL GROUP STANDS WEEPING
AT EVERY COTTAGE DOOR.

ALL THREE.
WE ARE COMING, FATHER ABR'AM,
THREE HUNDRED THOUSAND MORE!

(Music continues, underscoring appropriate to each vignette.)

INDIAN RECRUIT (CORDELIA). Chief Pug-o-na-ke-shick of the Chippewa Nation tenders the services of himself and his braves against the enemies of the country.

ITALIAN RECRUIT (LOVECRAFT). *(Italian dialect)* Greeting to you Abraham Lincoln, great pilot of freedom, from the Sons of Columbus!

GERMAN RECRUIT (TRUDGETT). *(German dialect)* I goes to fight mit Sigel!

(Caught up in the patriotic spirit, **THE FREEDMAN** *steps onto a platform, topping the music.)*

THE FREEDMAN. Hear me, brethren! Colored men whose fingers tingle to pull the trigger will not have to wait much longer. Be awake, therefore, brethren! A common patriotism, and a special call to defend your rights bid you to seize arms.

*(**THE SECRETARY** steps from the group, extremely embarrassed by what he must relay to **THE FREED-MAN**.)*

THE SECRETARY. The War Department has no intention – at *present* – to call any colored soldiers into the service.

THE FREEDMAN. *(stunned by the stupidity of it)* "Men! Men! Send us men!" they scream. What on earth is the matter with the American government? Do you really covet your own ruin? What are you thinking about? Or don't you condescend to think at all?

THE SECRETARY. The President is helpless in this. Arming the negroes would turn fifty thousand bayonets from the loyal border states against us.

THE FREEDMAN. *(acidly)* We were good enough to fight for George Washington. But we're not good enough to fight for George *McClellan*?

*(Everything stops. **THE SINGERS** consider this carefully for a moment. Then, having no good answer, they shrug and resume where they left off, exiting as they sing. Projection fades out.)*

THE NURSE & THE SOLDIER.
WE ARE COMING, WE ARE COMING,
OUR UNION TO RESTORE.

THE NURSE, THE SOLDIER & THE SECRETARY.
WE ARE COMING, FATHER ABR'AM,
WITH THREE HUNDRED THOUSAND MORE.
WE ARE COMING, FATHER ABR'AM,
WITH THREE HUNDRED THOUSAND MORE!

*(***THE FREEDMAN & THE GUIDE*** *are alone on stage.)*

THE FREEDMAN. *(lashing out)* The national edifice is on fire! Every man who can carry a bucket of water is wanted. Why does the government reject the negro? Is he not a man? Can he not wield a sword like any other? What blind, unreasoning prejudice!

THE GUIDE. *(with composure)* The "Good Time Coming" is almost here.

*(***THE FREEDMAN*** *laughs bitterly at the words and sings, his anger a sharp contrast to the music.)*

THE FREEDMAN.

NICODEMUS, THE SLAVE, WAS OF AFRICAN BIRTH,
AND WAS BOUGHT FOR A BAGFUL OF GOLD!
HE WAS RECKON'D AS PART OF THE SALT OF THE
 EARTH,
BUT HE DIED YEARS AGO, VERY OLD.
'TWAS HIS LAST SAD REQUEST – SO WE LAID HIM AWAY
IN THE TRUNK OF AN OLD HOLLOW TREE.
"WAKE ME UP!" WAS HIS CHARGE, "AT THE FIRST BREAK
 OF DAY –
WAKE ME UP FOR THE GREAT JUBILEE!"

THE FREEDMAN. *(cont.) (derisively)*

THE "GOOD TIME COMING" IS ALMOST HERE!

(He starts off, but she stops him.)

THE GUIDE. Two things I've got a right to, and these are death and liberty. One or the other I mean to have.

(She sings.)

HE WAS KNOWN AS A PROPHET – AT LEAST WAS AS
 WISE –
FOR HE TOLD OF THE BATTLES TO COME.
AND HE TREMBLED WITH DREAD WHEN HE ROLLED
 UP HIS EYES,

THE GUIDE. *(cont.)*

AND WE HEEDED THE SHAKE OF HIS THUMB.

THOUGH HE CLOTHED US WITH FEAR, YET THE
GARMENTS HE WORE

WERE IN PATCHES AT ELBOW AND KNEE.

AND HE STILL WEARS THE SUIT THAT HE USED TO OF
YORE,

AND HE SLEEPS IN THE OLD HOLLOW TREE!

(He joins her; there is a sweet hopefulness to the music now.)

BOTH.

THE "GOOD TIME COMING" IS ALMOST HERE!

IT WAS LONG, LONG, LONG ON THE WAY!

NOW RUN AND TELL ELIJAH TO HURRY UP POMP,

AND MEET US AT THE GUMTREE DOWN BY THE SWAMP,

TO WAKE NICODEMUS TODAY.

THE FREEDMAN.

'TWAS A LONG WEARY NIGHT – WE WERE ALMOST IN
FEAR

THAT THE FUTURE WAS MORE THAN HE KNEW!

'TWAS A LONG WEARY NIGHT – BUT THE MORNING IS
NEAR,

AND THE WORDS OF OUR PROPHET ARE TRUE.

THE GUIDE.

THERE ARE SIGNS IN THE SKY THAT THE DARKNESS IS
GONE –

THE FREEDMAN.

THERE ARE TOKENS IN ENDLESS ARRAY!

WHILE THE STORM, WHICH HAD SEEMINGLY
BANISHED THE DAWN,

ONLY HASTENS THE ADVENT OF DAY.

BOTH.

THE "GOOD TIME COMING" IS ALMOST HERE!

IT WAS LONG, LONG, LONG ON THE WAY!

NOW RUN AND TELL ELIJAH TO HURRY UP POMP,

AND MEET US AT THE GUMTREE DOWN BY THE SWAMP,

TO WAKE NICODEMUS TODAY.

(Lights down as they exit.)

PROJECTION (29):
"THE ENEMY IS
APPROACHING!"

*(***THE SECRETARY*** enters, fighting panic.)*

THE SECRETARY. Lee and his army have crossed the river into Maryland. His road now lies open to Washington, Philadelphia, New York – perhaps Boston!

(gives a look toward **MCCLELLAN***'s tent)*

For fortune tends to smile on a general with audacity!

(He dictates a telegram, his tone just this side of pleading.)

From the President. "My dear General McClellan: You must go after Lee. Please do not let him get off without being hurt."

(Lights down. He exits. Lights up on the exhausted **SOLDIER** *tramping in carrying his gear and rifle. He now wears a corporal's stripes. He collapses for a quick rest, but notices something on the ground. Curious, he reaches over and picks it up: a small packet of three cigars wrapped in a paper. Delighted with his luck, he unwraps them, sniffs approvingly, jams one in his mouth and fishes for a match. He is about to toss the paper away when curiosity gets the better of him. He reads, as* **HANNIBAL** *speaks the words.)*

HANNIBAL. "Headquarters, Army of Northern Virginia. Special Orders Number 191. Confidential. By command of…"

(He pauses, while **THE SOLDIER** *tries to make out the signature.)*

"General R.E. Lee."

(THE SOLDIER shrugs and crumples the paper. HANNIBAL clears his throat loudly to get his attention. THE SOLDIER looks at the paper again. HANNIBAL tries again.)

"General Robert E. *LEE.*"

(The importance finally dawning on him, THE SOLDIER leaps to his feet and runs off, waving the paper before him.)

THE SOLDIER. Sergeant! Sergeant!!

(Simultaneously, MCCLELLAN appears at his tent, a copy of the dispatch held high.)

MCCLELLAN. *(triumphantly)* To the President: I have all the plans of the Rebels and will catch them in their own trap. I think Lee has made a gross mistake and that he will be severely punished for it. My respects to Mrs. Lincoln.

(with a flourish)

Will send you trophies!

(He exits into tent.)

> *PROJECTION (30):*
> *"MR. LOVECRAFT IN*
> *'PAT MURPHY OF THE*
> *IRISH BRIGADE.'"*

(An IRISH MUSIC HALL TENOR (LOVECRAFT), steps into footlights and sings. The music grows progressively grimmer throughout, in counterpoint to the tenor's sentimentality.)

IRISH TENOR (LOVECRAFT)
SAYS PAT TO HIS MOTHER,
"IT LOOKS STRANGE TO SEE
BROTHERS FIGHTING IN SUCH A QUEER MANNER.
BUT I'LL FIGHT TILL I DIE, IF I NEVER GET KILLED,

FOR AMERICA'S BRIGHT STARRY BANNER."
FAR AWAY IN THE EAST WAS A DASHING YOUNG BLADE,
AND THE SONG HE WAS SINGING SO GAILY!
'TWAS HONEST PAT MURPHY OF THE IRISH BRIGADE
AND THE SONG OF THE SPLINTERED SHILLELAGH.
THE MORNING SOON BROKE AND POOR PADDY AWOKE
–
HE FOUND REBELS TO GIVE SATISFACTION.
AND THE DRUMMERS WERE BEATING THE DEVIL'S SAD
TUNE –
THEY WERE CALLING THE BOYS INTO ACTION!
FAR AWAY IN THE EAST WAS A DASHING YOUNG BLADE,
AND THE SONG HE WAS SINGING SO GAILY!
'TWAS HONEST PAT MURPHY OF THE IRISH BRIGADE
AND THE SONG OF THE SPLINTERED SHILLELAGH.

DISSOLVE TO PROJECTION (31):
CORPSES AT ANTIETAM.

(Music continues under as **THE SOLDIER** *enters,*
numbed by what he has been through.)

THE SOLDIER. A private from the Irish Brigade
appeared from the smoke, crying out for someone
to end his misery. Both of his eyes had been shot
out. Our lieutenant pressed his revolver against
the private's ear and pulled the trigger. The lieutenant turned to say something to us, but a cannon
ball took his head off.

IRISH TENOR.
SURE, THE DAY AFTER BATTLE THE DEAD LAY IN
HEAPS,
AND PAT MURPHY LAY BLEEDING AND GORY.
WITH A HOLE THROUGH HIS HEAD BY SOME ENEMY'S
BALL,
THAT ENDED HIS PASSION FOR GLORY.

(Music continues, as **THE NURSE** *enters wearily*
holding a lantern, a blood-spattered apron covering
her dress.)

THE NURSE. I found the ground literally covered with the dead and wounded. Most of the sufferers were from the Irish brigade. We could do little that night but distribute wine and tea, and speak comforting words. Then we sang. The sound stopped the shrieks and groans of the brave men. They listened. They all seemed comforted.

THE SOLDIER. *(confused)* All around me lay the Confederate dead. As I looked down on the poor, pinched faces, all enmity died out. There was no "secession" in those eyes staring blankly at the sky. It was not "their" war.

IRISH TENOR.

NO MORE IN THE CAMP WILL HIS LETTERS BE READ,
OR HIS SONG BE HEARD SINGING SO GAILY!
FOR HE DIED FAR AWAY FROM THE FRIENDS THAT HE
  LOVED,
AND FAR FROM THE LAND OF SHILLELAGH.
FAR AWAY IN THE EAST WAS A DASHING YOUNG BLADE,
AND THE SONG HE WAS SINGING SO GAILY!
'TWAS HONEST PAT MURPHY OF THE IRISH BRIGADE
AND THE SONG OF THE SPLINTERED SHILLELAGH.

(Lights down and all exit. Lights up on a jubilant
MCCLELLAN.*)*

MCCLELLAN. My Dearest Ellen: Those on whose judgment I rely tell me that I fought the battle splendidly and that it is a masterpiece of art. One of these days history will do me justice. "To the President: Maryland is entirely freed from the presence of the enemy."

(He sings.)

THE FLAG OF OUR COUNTRY IS FLOATING ON HIGH –
WE'LL STAND BY THAT FLAG TILL WE CONQUER OR
  DIE!
OUR CAUSE IS THE RIGHT ONE – OUR FOE'S IN THE
  WRONG!
FOR GOD AND FOR COUNTRY WE ARE MARCHING
  ALONG!

PROJECTION (32):
A GROUP OF SLAVES.

*(***THE FREEDMAN*** enters.)*

THE FREEDMAN. We strike at the effect, and leave the cause unharmed. Fire will not burn it out of us. Water cannot wash it out of us.

*(He exits. ***THE GUIDE*** enters.)*

THE GUIDE. Now, Mr. Lincoln, he's a great man, and I'm a poor nigger. But this nigger can tell Mr. Lincoln how to save the young men. He can do it by setting the niggers free. Suppose there was an awful big snake down there on the floor. He bites you. Folks are all scared, because you'll die. You send for a doctor to cut out the bite – but the snake is rolled up there. And while the doctor is doing it, he bites you again. The doctor cuts out that bite. But while he's doing it, the snake springs up and bites you again. And so he keeps doing. Till you kill him. That's what Mr. Lincoln ought to know.

*(***THE SECRETARY*** bursts in from the office.)*

THE SECRETARY. The Tycoon has stunned us all. He says God has decided the question – in favor of the slaves!

*(***THE FREEDMAN*** runs on, waving a folded newspaper.)*

THE FREEDMAN. Down Pennsylvania Avenue I ran as for my life! When the people saw me coming with the newspaper in my hand, they raised a cheer that was almost deafening. As many as could get around me lifted me to a great platform, and I started to read the proclamation.

(Laughing, as he tries to catch his breath.)

But I had run the best part of a mile – I was out of breath, and could not read….

(**THE GUIDE** *grabs the paper from him.*)

THE GUIDE. *(reads)* "On the first day of January, A.D. 1863…"

THE FREEDMAN. Men squealed, women fainted, dogs barked…

THE GUIDE. "…all persons held as slaves within any state in rebellion against the United States…"

THE FREEDMAN. White and colored people shook hands!

THE GUIDE. "…shall be then, thenceforward, and forever free."

THE FREEDMAN. It was indeed a time of times! And nothing like it will ever be seen again in this life!

THE GUIDE.

O, WASN'T THAT A WIDE RIVER,
THAT RIVER OF JORDAN, LORD,
WIDE RIVER!
THERE'S ONE MORE RIVER TO CROSS.

THE FREEDMAN & THE GUIDE.

O, WASN'T THAT A WIDE RIVER,
THAT RIVER OF JORDAN, LORD,
WIDE RIVER!
THERE'S ONE MORE RIVER TO CROSS.

(**THE SECRETARY, THE NURSE & THE SOLDIER** *enter carrying chairs. They seat themselves as a* **CONGREGATION** *in the following jubilant call-and-response.*)

THE GUIDE.

O, THE RIVER OF JORDAN IS SO WIDE!

COMPANY.

ONE MORE RIVER TO CROSS!

THE GUIDE.

I DON'T KNOW HOW TO GET ON THE OTHER SIDE!

COMPANY.

ONE MORE RIVER TO CROSS!

THE GUIDE.

OL' SATAN AIN'T NOTHIN' BUT A SNAKE IN THE GRASS!

COMPANY.

ONE MORE RIVER TO CROSS!

THE GUIDE.

IF YOU AIN'T MIGHTY CAREFUL HE WILL HOLD YOU
FAST!

COMPANY.

ONE MORE RIVER TO CROSS!

O, WASN'T THAT A WIDE RIVER,
THAT RIVER OF JORDAN, LORD,
WIDE RIVER!
THERE'S ONE MORE RIVER TO CROSS.

THE FREEDMAN.

JUST TELL US ALL ABOUT IT, NOW!

(Music continues under, as **THE GUIDE** *steps up on
level to testify.)*

THE GUIDE. Once the time was that I cried all night.
What's the matter? What's the matter? Matter
enough. The next morning my child was to be
sold. And she was sold. And I never expect to see
her till the Day of Judgment. Now – no more of
that. No more of that. No more of that. When I
went to the fields with my hands against my breast,
the overseer used to whip me along. Now, no
more of that. No more of that. No more of that,
now! President Lincoln has shut the gate!

THE FREEDMAN.

O, WASN'T THAT A WIDE RIVER,
THAT RIVER OF JORDAN, LORD,

COMPANY.

WIDE RIVER!
THERE'S ONE MORE RIVER TO CROSS.
O, WASN'T THAT A WIDE RIVER,
THAT RIVER OF JORDAN, LORD,
WIDE RIVER…

(Music stops as **MCCLELLAN** *bursts in from his tent in a rage, holding the newspaper up.)*

MCCLELLAN. This proclamation is infamous! My fight is to save the Union, not to end slavery. If they think I will see my brave men's blood shed for their radical schemes, they are badly mistaken!

*(***THE SOLDIER*** steps front and speaks quietly but firmly.)*

THE SOLDIER. I've never been in favor of the abolition of slavery. But this war has determined me in the conviction that it is a greater sin than we are able to stand. So now I go in for a war of emancipation – and I am ready and willing to do my share of the work.

(Caught off-guard, **MCCLELLAN** *covers his tracks awkwardly, trying to salvage a scrap of dignity.)*

MCCLELLAN. My advisors are of the opinion that it is my duty to submit to the President's proclamation. I presume they are right.

(He exits into tent. **THE FREEDMAN & THE GUIDE** *exit.)*

THE SECRETARY. We are hereafter a nation of soldiers!

THE NURSE. This is God's war now – no soul can stand on neutral ground!

THE SECRETARY.
SO WE'RE SPRINGING TO THE CALL
FROM THE EAST AND FROM THE WEST,
SHOUTING THE BATTLE CRY OF FREEDOM.
AND WE'LL HURL THE REBEL CREW
FROM THE LAND WE LOVE THE BEST,
SHOUTING THE BATTLE CRY OF FREEDOM.

THE SECRETARY, THE NURSE & THE SOLDIER.
THE UNION FOREVER,
HURRAH, BOYS, HURRAH!
DOWN WITH THE TRAITOR,

UP WITH THE STAR!
WHILE WE RALLY 'ROUND THE FLAG, BOYS,
RALLY ONCE AGAIN,
SHOUTING THE BATTLE CRY OF FREEDOM!

THE SOLDIER.

WE ARE SPRINGING TO THE CALL
OF OUR BROTHERS GONE BEFORE,
SHOUTING THE BATTLE CRY OF FREEDOM.
AND WE'LL FILL THE VACANT RANKS
WITH A MILLION FREEMEN MORE,
SHOUTING THE BATTLE CRY OF FREEDOM.

THE SECRETARY, THE NURSE & THE SOLDIER.

THE UNION FOREVER,
HURRAH, BOYS, HURRAH!
DOWN WITH THE TRAITOR,
UP WITH THE STAR!
WHILE WE RALLY 'ROUND THE FLAG, BOYS,
RALLY ONCE AGAIN,
SHOUTING THE BATTLE CRY OF FREEDOM!

*(***THE THREE OF THEM*** step upstage. ***THE GUIDE***
helps ***THE FREEDMAN*** exchange his coat for a
Union private's blouse. He picks up a rifle, and she
crowns him with an infantryman's forage cap. He
stands as if posing for a photograph.)*

THE GUIDE.

HOLD OUT YOUR LIGHT,
YOU HEAV'N BOUND SOLDIER!
HOLD OUT YOUR LIGHT,
YOU HEAV'N BOUND SOLDIER!
HOLD OUT YOUR LIGHT,
YOU HEAV'N BOUND SOLDIER!
LET YOUR LIGHT SHINE AROUND THE WORLD.

PROJECTION (33):
PHOTO OF THE
FREEDMAN IN UNIFORM.

THE GUIDE. *(cont.)*

    O, DEACON, CAN'T YOU HOLD OUT YOUR LIGHT?
    O, DEACON, CAN'T YOU HOLD OUT YOUR LIGHT?
    O, DEACON, CAN'T YOU HOLD OUT YOUR LIGHT?
    LET YOUR LIGHT SHINE AROUND THE WORLD.

> *PROJECTION (34):*
> *DISSOLVE INTO PHOTO*
> *OF A LONG LINE OF*
> *BLACK UNION SOLDIERS.*

THE GUIDE & THE FREEDMAN.

    HOLD OUT YOUR LIGHT,
    YOU HEAV'N BOUND SOLDIER!
    HOLD OUT YOUR LIGHT,
    YOU HEAV'N BOUND SOLDIER!
    HOLD OUT YOUR LIGHT,
    YOU HEAV'N BOUND SOLDIER!
    LET YOUR LIGHT SHINE AROUND THE WORLD.

THE SOLDIER.

    WE WILL WELCOME TO OUR NUMBERS THE LOYAL,
        TRUE, AND BRAVE!

THE SECRETARY, THE NURSE & THE SOLDIER.

    SHOUTING THE BATTLE CRY OF FREEDOM!

THE NURSE.

    AND ALTHOUGH HE MAY BE POOR, NOT A MAN SHALL
        BE A SLAVE!

THE SECRETARY, THE NURSE & THE SOLDIER.

    SHOUTING THE BATTLE CRY OF FREEDOM.

THE GUIDE & THE FREEDMAN.

    HEAV'N BOUND SOLDIER!
    LET YOUR LIGHT SHINE, SOLDIER!
    HEAV'N BOUND SOLDIER!

THE SECRETARY, THE NURSE & THE SOLDIER.

    THE UNION FOREVER,
    HURRAH, BOYS, HURRAH!
    DOWN WITH THE TRAITOR,

UP WITH THE STAR!
WHILE WE RALLY 'ROUND THE FLAG, BOYS,
RALLY ONCE AGAIN,
SHOUTING THE BATTLE CRY OF FREEDOM!

THE GUIDE & THE FREEDMAN. *(counterpoint)*

HOLD OUT YOUR LIGHT,
YOU HEAV'N BOUND SOLDIER!
HOLD OUT YOUR LIGHT,
YOU HEAV'N BOUND SOLDIER!
HOLD OUT YOUR LIGHT,
YOU HEAV'N BOUND SOLDIER!
LET YOUR LIGHT SHINE AROUND THE WORLD!

(During the above, **MCCLELLAN** *steps out of his tent and makes the decision to join the group, as* **THE COMPANY** *sings in unison.)*

COMPANY.

THE UNION FOREVER!
HURRAH, BOYS, HURRAH!
DOWN WITH THE TRAITOR,
UP WITH THE STAR!
WHILE WE RALLY 'ROUND THE FLAG, BOYS,
RALLY ONCE AGAIN,
SHOUTING THE BATTLE CRY OF FREEDOM!

PROJECTION (35):
TITLE SLIDE.

(Blackout)

End Act I

ACT II

PROJECTION (35):
TITLE SLIDE.

(Music: fanfare. Light up on **HAWK**.*)*

HAWK. *(with gravity)* We welcome you back, honored guests, as we return to the capital, gripped by the cold hand of war. *(Brightening)* But first! A popular diversion performed to great acclaim from discriminating theatregoers during the years in which our story is set.

(A gesture toward the conductor.)

Maestro, if you would be so kind?

(MUSIC in: "DER DEITCHER'S DOG.")

PROJECTION (36):
"MR. TRUDGETT,
MISS HOPEWELL &
MR. HAWK IN
'DER DEITCHER'S DOG.'"

(Footlights up and an **IMMIGRANT BOY (TRUDGETT)** *clomps in wearing a ludicrous Teutonic getup, elaborately searching for something. He sings in thick bogus German dialect.)*

BOY.

OH VERE, OH VERE IS MINE LITTLE DOG GONE?
OH VERE, OH VERE CAN HE BE?

(He crosses to the beer hall **WAITRESS (CORDELIA)**.*)*

67

BOY. *(cont.)*

HIS EARS CUT SHORT UND HIS TAIL CUT LONG?

(She shrugs.)

OH VERE, OH VERE IS HE?

*(**BUTCHER (HAWK)** has entered.)*

ALL 3.

TRA LA LA LA LA LA LA LA LA LA LA,

LA LA LA LA LA LA LA LA LA LA,

TRA LA LA LA LA LA LA LA LA LA LA,

TRA LA LA LA LA LA LA.

*(They continue in dumb show, as **THE SECRETARY** turns to us from his chair, aghast at the drivel he is being forced to watch.)*

THE SECRETARY. All our theaters are open and all are crowded nightly. The kind of entertainment seems to be of little account to people. If the prices are high and the place is fashionable, nothing more is required.

*(**WAITRESS** dangles a beer stein seductively toward **THE BOY**.)*

BOY

I LOVES MINE LAGER –

WAITRESS.

'TIS VERY GOOT BEER!

BOY

OH VERE, OH VERE CAN HE BE?

*(Hopefully, to **WAITRESS**.)*

BUT MIT NO MONEY?

WAITRESS. *(yanking it away)*

YOU CANNOT DRINK HERE!

BOY. *(bawling)*

OH VERE, OH VERE IS HE?

ALL 3.

> TRA LA LA LA LA LA LA LA LA LA LA,
> LA LA LA LA LA LA LA LA LA LA,
> TRA LA LA LA LA LA LA LA LA LA LA,
> TRA LA LA LA LA LA LA.

THE SECRETARY. *(disgusted)* This war has entirely changed the American character. A man can sell almost anything to the government at any price he has the courage to ask. And the one who makes the most money – no matter how – and spends the most money – no matter for what – is considered the greatest man.

> *(***THE BUTCHER*** *whistles to get* ***THE BOY***'s *attention. He holds up a good-sized string of sausages.)*

BOY.

> UND ZAUSAGE IS GOOT!

> *(He points to the sausage.)*

> Baloney?

BUTCHER. *(proudly)* Of course!

BOY.

> OH VERE, OH VERE CAN HE BE?

WAITRESS. *(referring to* ***THE BUTCHER***)

> DEY MAKES 'EM MIT DOG!
> UND DEY MAKES 'EM MIT HORSE!

> *(Elaborate take from* ***THE BOY***.*)*

BOY. *(front)* I guess dey makes 'em mit he!

> *(Bedlam, as* ***THE BOY*** *chases* ***THE BUTCHER*** *to retrieve the sausage.)*

ALL 3.

> TRA LA LA LA LA LA LA LA LA LA LA,
> LA LA LA LA LA LA LA LA LA LA,
> TRA LA LA LA LA LA LA LA LA LA LA,
> TRA LA LA LA LA LA LA.

THE SECRETARY. The world has seen its iron age, its silver age, and its golden age. This is the age of shoddy.

ALL 3.

TRA LA LA LA LA LA LA!

(Blackout.)

PROJECTION (37):
ANTIETAM CASUALTY LIST.

(Lights up. It is late summer, oppressively hot. **THE FREEDWOMAN** *enters.)*

PROJECTION (38):
CONFEDERATE GENERAL
STONEWALL JACKSON.

THE FREEDWOMAN. Mr. Lincoln watches our army with agonizing impatience, while he speaks in the highest terms of such brave Southern generals as Lee and Stonewall Jackson. Mr. Lincoln has often said General Jackson is his ideal soldier. "What a pity we should have to fight such a gallant fellow," he said. "If only we had such a man to lead the armies of the North!"

THE SECRETARY. The country groans but nothing is done. I am beginning to think McClellan's game now is to maintain a stalemate that will save slavery, and make himself the next President.

*(***MCCLELLAN** *enters from tent.)*

MCCLELLAN. I doubt that Napoleon ever possessed the love of his men more fully than I do.

THE SECRETARY. *(confidentially)* The Tycoon thinks McClellan is – a little crazy. He says, "It isn't the Army of the Potomac – it's McClellan's body-guard."

(Lights and music change to suggest autumn.)

PROJECTION (39):
PHOTO OF LINCOLN
FACING MCCLELLAN.

He felt the need to pay a visit to The Young Napoleon.

MCCLELLAN. The President was very affable. I really think he feels very kindly towards me personally...

THE SECRETARY. The Tycoon told him he would be a ruined man if he didn't move...

MCCLELLAN. *(oblivious)* He is convinced I am the best general in the country...

THE SECRETARY. *(exploding)* It requires the lever of Archimedes to move this inert mass!

(He forces himself to stay calm by adopting an exquisitely diplomatic tone with the general.)

THE SECRETARY. *(cont.)* Major General McClellan: The President directs that you cross the Potomac and give battle to the enemy. He is...very desirous that your army move as soon as possible."

(After considering this for a moment, **MCCLELLAN** *crosses to his tent and sits. Music and lights change: winter.)*

MCCLELLAN. *(maddeningly unhurried)* I urgently request more horses. Mine are broken down with fatigue.

THE SECRETARY. *(acidly)* From the President: "Will you pardon me for asking what the horses of your army have done since the battle of Antietam that would fatigue anything?"

(Music stops abruptly. **MCCLELLAN** *rises angrily.)*

MCCLELLAN. It was one of those dirty little flings that I can't get used to when they are not merited. He would relieve me tomorrow – if he dared. His cowardice alone prevents it.

(A tense silence. Finally:)

THE SECRETARY. By direction of the President, it is ordered that Major General McClellan be relieved from the command of the Army of the Potomac...

(Stunned, **MCCLELLAN** *moves toward* **THE SECRETARY,** *as* **HANNIBAL** *enters.)*

MCCLELLAN. The Army of the Potomac is my army! We have grown together and fought together. We are wedded and must not be separated!

*(***THE SECRETARY** *is enjoying this a lot less than he expected. To* **HANNIBAL.***)*

THE SECRETARY. "...and that Major General Burnside take the command."

(Drumroll. **HANNIBAL** *replaces* **MCCLELLAN** *'s portrait with a portait of General Ambrose Burnside. MUSIC under: "MARCHING ALONG," slowly.* **THE SOLDIER** *enters as* **THE SECRETARY** *and* **HANNIBAL** *exit.)*

THE SOLDIER. We stood at attention, and for the best part of three miles we could hear the cheers, coming closer and closer. When Little Mac finally appeared, I can tell you we gave him three rousing cheers of our own.

(Sound: train whistle blast. **MCCLELLAN** *steps up on platform to face his army, trying to master his emotions.* **THE SOLDIER** *faces him at attention.)*

MCCLELLAN. I cannot express the love and gratitude I bear to you. You have grown up under my care....

THE SOLDIER. *(grimly, to us)* The officers whisper of marching on Washington to seize the government.

MCCLELLAN. *(lifting his cap)* To the Army of the Potomac! And bless the day when I shall return to it.

THE SOLDIER. *(as before)* One word, one look of encouragement, the lifting of a finger would be a signal for a revolt by the Army of the Potomac.

(He turns back to **MCCLELLAN***, watching for a sign. Finally* **MCCLELLAN** *speaks – his finest moment.)*

MCCLELLAN. Stand by General Burnside as you have stood by me, and all will be well.

(Sound: another blast from the train whistle, and **MCCLELLAN** *exits.)*

> *PROJECTION (40): "*
> *ON TO RICHMOND!"*

*(*THE FREEDWOMAN *enters.)*

THE FREEDWOMAN. Fredericksburg.

(Music: a grim chord from the pit.)

> *PROJECTION (41):*
> *FREDERICKSBURG.*

THE SOLDIER. We might as well have tried to take Hell.

(He exits. **THE SECRETARY** *enters quietly from the office.)*

THE SECRETARY. If there's a worse place than Hell, the Tycoon is in it.

(Drumroll. **HANNIBAL** *replaces Burnside's portrait with General Joseph Hooker's.)*

From the President. "General Hooker: I have heard of your saying that the government needed a dictator. Of course it was not for this, but in spite of it, that I have given you the command. Only those generals who gain successes can set up dictators. What I now ask of you is military success, and I will risk the dictatorship."

THE FREEDWOMAN. *(simply, sadly)* Chancellorsville.

(Music: chord, as before.)

> *PROJECTION (42):*
> *CORPSES AT*
> *CHANCELLORSVILLE.*

THE SECRETARY. *(stunned)* My God, my God – what will the country say? 130,000 magnificent soldiers cut to pieces by 60,000 half-starved ragamuffins!

(Drumroll. **HANNIBAL** *replaces Hooker's portrait with General George Meade's.* **THE SECRETARY** *continues with a tired sigh.)*

"To General –"

(He gropes to remember who comes next – finally looks to **HANNIBAL** *for help.)*

HANNIBAL. *(gently)* Meade.

THE SECRETARY. *(nodding)* Meade. "General Meade: This order places you in command of the Army of the Potomac."

(He exits slowly into office.)

HANNIBAL. *(a nod at Meade's portrait)* He says he's been condemned without a trial.

THE FREEDWOMAN. Gettysburg.

*(***THE GUIDE & HANNIBAL** *exit.)*

> *PROJECTION (43):*
> *THE BODY-STREWN*
> *FIELD OF GETTYSBURG.*

*(***MEN** *sing quietly offstage.* **THE NURSE** *enters and speaks over the singing.)*

MEN.

> THE STARS ABOVE IN HEAVEN NOW ARE LOOKING KINDLY DOWN,
> THE STARS ABOVE IN HEAVEN NOW ARE LOOKING KINDLY DOWN,
> THE STARS ABOVE IN HEAVEN NOW ARE LOOKING KINDLY DOWN,
> ON THE GRAVE OF OLD JOHN BROWN.

THE NURSE. The field was covered with the slain; the full moon looked down with serene luster on the field of Gettysburg, trodden down for miles by the two great armies. Cheer after cheer rose from the triumphant boys in blue, echoing from Round Top, re-echoing from Cemetery Hill, and making the very heavens throb. Here and there the men began to sing, "John Brown's Soul." The song swept weirdly over the bloody field.

(She turns upstage for a moment, listening.)

MEN.
GLORY, GLORY, HALLELUJAH,
GLORY, GLORY, HALLELUJAH,
GLORY, GLORY, HALLELUJAH,
HIS SOUL GOES MARCHING ON.

> *PROJECTION (44):*
> *DISSOLVE TO PHOTO*
> *OF WOUNDED OUTSIDE*
> *A FIELD HOSPITAL.*

*(**THE NURSE** exits wearily upstage, toward the projection.)*

> *PROJECTION (45):*
> *DISSOLVE TO PHOTO*
> *OF A HOSPITAL WARD.*

*(MUSIC: "JOHN BROWN'S BODY" resolves into the gentle 3/4 accompaniment for "SOMEBODY'S DARLING." **THE FREEDWOMAN** appears in the window.)*

THE FREEDWOMAN.
INTO THE WARD OF THE CLEAN WHITEWASHED HALLS,
WHERE THE DEAD SLEPT AND THE DYING LAY;
WOUNDED BY BAYONETS, SABRES AND BALLS,
SOMEBODY'S DARLING WAS BORNE ONE DAY....

*(Music continues under. **THE NURSE** re-enters, carrying a wash basin and bandages. She rolls bandages as she speaks.)*

THE NURSE. One evening, I found a bed occupied by a large, fair man, with a fine face, and the serenest eyes I ever met. As John lay high upon his pillows, no picture of dying statesman or warrior was ever fuller of real dignity than this blacksmith. He seemed to cling to life, as if it were rich in duties and delights. I wrote the letter which he dictated. As I sealed it, he said, "I hope the answer will come in time for me to see it."

THE FREEDWOMAN.

SOMEBODY'S DARLING,
SO YOUNG AND SO BRAVE,
WEARING STILL ON HIS SWEET YET PALE FACE –
SOON TO BE HID IN THE DUST OF THE GRAVE –
THE LINGERING LIGHT OF HIS BOYHOOD'S GRACE.

THE NURSE. Now John was dying, and the letter had not come. I had been summoned to many death beds, but to none that made my heart ache as it did then. As I went in, he stretched out both hands: "I knew you'd come! I guess I'm moving on, ma'am." He was. I sat down by him and waited to help him die. He stood in sore need of help – and I could do so little...

THE FREEDWOMAN

SOMEBODY'S WATCHING AND WAITING FOR HIM,
YEARNING TO HOLD HIM AGAIN TO HER BREAST;
YET, THERE HE LIES WITH HIS BLUE EYES SO DIM,
AND PURPLE, CHILD-LIKE LIPS HALF APART.
TENDERLY BURY THE FAIR, UNKNOWN DEAD,
PAUSING TO DROP ON HIS GRAVE A TEAR;
CARVE ON THE WOODEN SLAB OVER HIS HEAD,
"SOMEBODY'S DARLING IS SLUMBERING HERE."

(Music continues under.)

THE NURSE. He never spoke again, but to the end held my hand so close that when he was asleep at last, I could not draw it away. As I stood looking at him, the ward master handed me a letter, saying it had been forgotten the night before. It was John's letter, come just an hour too late. I laid the letter in his hand. Then I left the brave Virginia blacksmith, as he lay serenely waiting for the dawn of that long day which knows no night.

(She starts off, but turns back.)

THE FREEDWOMAN.
SOMEBODY'S DARLING, SOMEBODY'S PRIDE.

THE FREEDWOMAN & THE NURSE.
WHO'LL TELL HIS MOTHER
WHERE HER BOY DIED?

(Music and lights down as they exit. Lights up on **THE SECRETARY**, *addressing the unseen press, in upbeat, official mode.)*

THE SECRETARY. The President directs me to announce a great success to the cause of the Union at Gettysburg!

(Confidentially to us, worried.)

But the enemy is driving every able-bodied man into his ranks, as a butcher drives cattle into a slaughter pen. We can do no less.

(A pause while he puts off the inevitable. But he can't avoid saying it.)

We must have more troops.

> *PROJECTION (46):*
> *HEADLINE: "THE DRAFT."*

Tomorrow the first draft in New York City will be held. God knows how the upstanding citizens of that nest of treason will respond to a draft.

> *PROJECTION (47):*
> *"SUBSTITUTE*
> *WANTED" AD.*

(Lights up on the **SUBSTITUTE BROKER (HANNI-BAL)**, *who calls out like a carnival barker.)*

SUBSTITUTE BROKER (HANNIBAL). Substitutes wanted! Three hundred dollars cash paid! Step right up! Draft substitutes bought and sold!

> *PROJECTION (48):*
> *"MR. HAWK, MR. TRUDGETT*
> *& MR. DRUMWRIGHT IN*
> *'GRAFTED INTO THE ARMY.'"*

(MUSIC: "GRAFTED INTO THE ARMY.")

(Lights up on **THE WIDOW (HAWK**, *wearing a ridiculous Mother Hubbard dress, bonnet and granny glasses) leaning on a cane. This is played as a corny music hall number.)*

THE WIDOW (HAWK).

OUR JIMMY HAS GONE FOR TO LIVE IN A TENT –
THEY HAVE GRAFTED HIM INTO THE ARMY!
HE FINALLY PUCKERED UP COURAGE AND WENT,
WHEN THEY GRAFTED HIM INTO THE ARMY.

(He reaches offstage with his cane. When he pulls it back, it is attached to an unhappy-looking **DRAFTEE (TRUDGETT)**, *in an oversized uniform coat and cap.)*

I TOLD THEM THE CHILD WAS TOO YOUNG, ALAS!
AT THE CAPTAIN'S FOREQUARTERS,
THEY SAID HE WOULD PASS!
THEY'D TRAIN HIM UP WELL IN THE INFANTRY CLASS –

DRAFTEE (TRUDGETT).

THEY GRAFTED ME INTO THE ARMY!

THE WIDOW.

OH, JIMMY, FAREWELL!
YOUR BROTHERS FELL WAY DOWN IN ALABARMY!
I THOUGHT THEY WOULD SPARE A LONE WIDDER'S
    HEIR,

DRAFTEE.

BUT THEY GRAFTED ME INTO THE ARMY!

(During the next verse, **THE SUBSTITUTE BROKER** *pulls out a knapsack, haversack and rifle out of a trunk, dumping them in* **THE DRAFTEE**'s *unwilling arms.)*

THE WIDOW.

NOW IN MY PROVISIONS I SEE HIM REVEALED –

DRAFTEE.

THEY'VE GRAFTED ME INTO THE ARMY!

THE WIDOW.

A PICKET BESIDE THE CONTENTED FIELD.

DRAFTEE.

THEY GRAFTED ME INTO THE ARMY!

THE WIDOW.

HE LOOKS KINDER SICKISH – BEGINS TO CRY!
A BIG VOLUNTEER STANDING RIGHT IN HIS EYE!
OH, WHAT IF THE DUCKY SHOULD UP AND DIE?

DRAFTEE.

NOW THEY'VE GRAFTED ME INTO THE ARMY!

(During the chorus, **THE OLD WIDOW** *pushes* **THE DRAFTEE** *on his way, waving a hanky after him in a show of sorrow. The hapless* **DRAFTEE** *shambles off into the wings, rifle dragging behind him.)*

THE WIDOW.

OH, JIMMY, FAREWELL!
YOUR BROTHERS FELL WAY DOWN IN ALABARMY!
I THOUGHT THEY WOULD SPARE A LONE WIDDER'S
   HEIR –

*(***THE WIDOW** *holds out a hand expectantly to* **THE SUBSTITUTE BROKER**, *who places a fat wad of bills in it. she drops the money into her roomy bodice.)*

THE BROKER & THE WIDOW.

BUT THEY GRAFTED HIM INTO THE ARMY!

(The bright play-off is interrupted by a crash of broken glass.)

> *PROJECTION (49):*
> *HEADLINE –*
> *"THE MOB IN NEW YORK."*

RIOTER (TRUDGETT). *(shouted from offstage)* The rich man's money and the poor man's blood!

*(***THE FREEDWOMAN*** enters.)*

> *PROJECTION (49.1):*
> *ENGRAVING OF RIOTERS*
> *ON RAMPAGE.*

THE FREEDWOMAN. For three days, gangs of men and boys, the scum of the city, broke into stores, hotels and saloons, and marched through every part of New York City. Having been taught to hate the negro, the mob paid special visits to all localities inhabited by blacks. The mobs were led on with loud cheers for General McClellan.

*(Lights up on ***THE SECRETARY*** at the office door.)*

THE SECRETARY. That name again! Gettysburg is a dreadful reminiscence of McClellan. Think of it – we had the rebels within our grasp. We had only to stretch out our hands and they were ours. But the army would not move. Now General Meade says he's driven the invader from our soil. Will they never get that idea out of their heads? The whole country is our soil! We must have a general somewhere who understands what is required.

*(***THE FREEDMAN*** enters, back in uniform.)*

> *PROJECTION (50):*
> *GENERAL ULYSSES GRANT*
> *IN FIELD UNIFORM,*
> *LEANING AGAINST A TREE.*

THE FREEDMAN. *(speaking Grant's words)* "The art of war is simple enough. Find out where your enemy is. Get at him as soon as you can. Strike at him as hard as you can and as often as you can. And keep moving on. General Ulysses S. Grant."

> *PROJECTION (51):*
> *DISSOLVE TO CLOSE-UP*
> *OF GRANT IN DRESS*
> *UNIFORM.*

THE SECRETARY. "From the President: General Grant will henceforth command all our armies."

(Drumroll. **HANNIBAL** *replaces Meade's portrait with Grant's. He hands a dispatch to* **THE SECRETARY.***)*

THE FREEDMAN. "From General Grant: General Sherman will move on Atlanta. I propose to fight it out on this line – if it takes all summer."

(He nods approvingly at Grant's portrait.)

The boss has arrived.

*(***THE FREEDWOMAN*** enters.)*

THE FREEDWOMAN. Mrs. Lincoln cannot tolerate General Grant. She says he is a butcher and she could fight an army as well herself. His tactics are simply to march a new line of men up to be shot down as fast as they take their position, and to keep marching until the enemy grows tired of the slaughter.

THE SECRETARY. He isn't shrieking for reinforcements all the time. He takes what we can give him and does the best he can with what he's got.

(enthusiastically)

"From the President. Lieutenant General Grant: Hold on with a bull-dog grip, and chew and choke, as much as possible."

> *PROJECTION (52):*
> *"18,000 FALL IN*
> *THE WILDERNESS."*
>
> *PROJECTION (53):*
> *DISSOLVE TO A*
> *SHOCKINGLY CARE-WORN*
> *LINCOLN.*

THE FREEDWOMAN. The people are wild for peace –

THE SECRETARY. They expect too much! This war is eating his life out.

(**ALL** *exit. Lights up on* **HOMETOWN GIRL***, who is seated, writing a letter. She has a small photo case to which she refers during the song. During the first verse,* **THE SOLDIER** *enters opposite, quietly drops his knapsack and rifle, and seats himself to write a letter. He now wears a sergeant's stripes.*)

HOMETOWN GIRL (CORDELIA).

DEAREST LOVE, DO YOU REMEMBER, WHEN WE LAST
    DID MEET,
HOW YOU TOLD ME THAT YOU LOVED ME, KNEELING
    AT MY FEET?
OH! HOW PROUD YOU STOOD BEFORE ME IN YOUR
    SUIT OF BLUE,
WHEN YOU VOWED TO ME AND COUNTRY EVER TO BE
    TRUE.

HOMETOWN GIRL & THE SOLDIER.

WEEPING SAD AND LONELY,
HOPES AND FEARS HOW VAIN!

THE SOLDIER.

YET PRAYING,

HOMETOWN GIRL.

WHEN THIS CRUEL WAR IS OVER,

HOMETOWN GIRL & THE SOLDIER.

PRAYING THAT WE MEET AGAIN!

*(**THE FREEDMAN** and **ANOTHER SOLDIER (LOVE-
CRAFT)** enter quietly during the following. They sit
near **THE SOLDIER** and take up pencil and paper
and start their own letters.)*

HOMETOWN GIRL & THE SOLDIER.

WHEN THE SUMMER BREEZE IS SIGHING MOURNFULLY
    ALONG;
OR WHEN AUTUMN LEAVES ARE FALLING, SADLY
    BREATHES THE SONG.

HOMETOWN GIRL.

OFT IN DREAMS I SEE THEE LYING ON THE BATTLE
    PLAIN,
LONELY, WOUNDED, EVEN DYING, CALLING – BUT IN
    VAIN.

(Music continues under.)

THE SOLDIER. *(reading over what he has written)* As I was
running past a wounded rebel, he caught me by
the pant leg and held me so tight I had to beat his
hand loose with my gun. He wanted me to help
him off the field.

THE FREEDMAN. *(the same)* It is not for us to blow our
horn, but when a regiment of white men gave us
three cheers, it shows that we did our duty.

THE SOLDIER. Our regiment's ranks does not number
a hundred men now. Six weeks ago she numbered
eight hundred and sixty-seven.

THE FREEDMAN. The loss in our brigade was hot and
heavy.

THE SOLDIER.

WE'VE BEEN FIGHTING TODAY ON THE OLD CAMP
    GROUND,
MANY ARE LYING NEAR.
SOME ARE DEAD AND SOME ARE DYING,
MANY ARE IN TEARS.

*(The other **SOLDIERS** join in, including **HAWK**
from offstage.)*

MEN.

> MANY ARE THE HEARTS THAT ARE WEARY TONIGHT,
> WISHING FOR THE WAR TO CEASE;

THE SOLDIER.

> MANY ARE THE HEARTS THAT ARE LOOKING FOR THE
>   RIGHT
> TO SEE THE DAWN OF PEACE.

MEN.

> TENTING TONIGHT, TENTING TONIGHT,
> TENTING ON THE OLD CAMP GROUND.

> *(Music continues under.)*

THE SOLDIER. *(grimly)* I pray God that I may pull the rope to hang Jeff Davis – for still carrying on this wicked and cruel war and keeping me from my dear ones.

THE FREEDMAN. I will now close my letter, for there is neither pen, paper, ink, nor pencil that can describe the desolation of war.

> *(***THE SOLDIERS*** *pin their letters to the insides of their coats.)*

THE SOLDIER. If I am slain, whoever finds this letter will please to state the fact in this and forward it.

> *(Near the breaking point, he rises angrily.)*

> WE ARE TIRED OF WAR ON THE OLD CAMP GROUND!
> MANY ARE DEAD AND GONE,
> OF THE BRAVE AND TRUE WHO'VE LEFT THEIR HOMES
>   –
> OTHERS BEEN WOUNDED LONG.

MEN.

> MANY ARE THE HEARTS THAT ARE WEARY TONIGHT,
> WISHING FOR THE WAR TO CEASE;

THE SOLDIER.

> MANY ARE THE HEARTS THAT ARE LOOKING FOR THE
>   RIGHT

MEN.

TO SEE THE DAWN OF PEACE!
DYING TONIGHT, DYING TONIGHT,
DYING ON THE OLD CAMP GROUND.

(Light up on **THE GIRL,** *clutching her photo.)*

HOMETOWN GIRL.

BUT OUR COUNTRY CALLED YOU, DARLING – ANGELS
    CHEER YOUR WAY!
WHILE OUR NATION'S SONS ARE FIGHTING, WE CAN
    ONLY PRAY.
NOBLY STRIKE FOR GOD AND LIBERTY! LET ALL
    NATIONS SEE
HOW WE LOVE THE STARRY BANNER, EMBLEM OF THE
    FREE.

*(***THE SOLDIER*** takes out his photo case as he sings.
They cross toward each other.)*

BOTH.

WEEPING SAD AND LONELY,

HOMETOWN GIRL

HOPES AND FEARS HOW VAIN!

THE SOLDIER.

YET PRAYING,

BOTH.

WHEN THIS CRUEL WAR IS OVER,
PRAYING THAT WE MEET AGAIN!

*(***THE HOMETOWN GIRL & THE SOLDIER*** exit.
MCCLELLAN strides into light.)*

MCCLELLAN. It is my firm conviction that no man
should seek the Presidency.

(He steps up onto platform.)

And that no true man should refuse it.

> *PROJECTION (54):*
> *"MCCLELLAN FOR*
> *PRESIDENT" POSTER.*

*(***THE FREEDWOMAN*** enters.)*

THE FREEDWOMAN. General McClellan was nominated unanimously by the Democrats. Cheers, yells, music, and screams rent the air, and cannon volleyed a salute in honor of the nominee.

(She exits. **THE SECRETARY & HANNIBAL** *enter with a newspaper. Music under the rapid-fire exchange.)*

HANNIBAL. The papers are full of McClellan!

THE SECRETARY. *(reading from newspaper)* "Elect Lincoln and you will bring on negro equality…"

HANNIBAL. *(reading from same newspaper)* "Elect McClellan and you will defeat negro equality…"

THE SECRETARY. "…harder times…"

HANNIBAL. "…restore prosperity…"

THE SECRETARY. "…universal anarchy…"

HANNIBAL. "…and re-establish the union…"

THE SECRETARY. "…and ultimate ruin!"

HANNIBAL. "…in an honorable and happy peace!"

*(***TRUDGETT & CORDELIA*** *enter and face* **MCCLELLAN,** *as* **ADORING SUPPORTERS.***)*

MCCLELLAN. The only essential for peace is a restoration of the Union.

HANNIBAL. He says nothing of preserving emancipation.

*(***THE SECRETARY*** *crosses to the office door.)*

MCCLELLAN. We are not for wading through seas of blood to reorganize the whole social structure of the South.

(Music out. **THE SECRETARY** *reads from a letter, his spirits at their lowest.)*

THE SECRETARY. "Confidential. From the President. This morning, as for some days past, it seems exceedingly probable that this Administration will not be re-elected."

HANNIBAL. Lincoln is deader than dead.

THE SECRETARY. It is now four months since General Sherman started for Atlanta. The people must have this victory – without it, they will not find the stomach to finish this war. Is all this blood to go for nothing?

MCCLELLAN. The political news is all favorable. We are quite confident of the outcome.

*(**THE GUIDE** runs in waving a dispatch.)*

THE GUIDE (CASSIE). From General Sherman! "Atlanta is ours, and fairly won."

*(As this stunning news sinks in, **TRUDGETT &** **CORDELIA** join the others, leaving **MCCLELLAN** standing by himself.)*

THE SECRETARY. *(ecstatic)* To General Sherman. "My Dear General: Many thanks." *(pause)* "Would be pleased if you could furlough as many soldiers as possible to go home and vote."

THE SOLDIER. Little Mac is for letting them have their slaves. Then we can fight them again in ten years. But let Old Abe settle it, and it's always settled.

THE SECRETARY. *(nervously)* Dispatches have been coming in all evening...

HANNIBAL. Electoral votes: Lincoln, 212. McClellan – 21!

PROJECTION (55):
"LINCOLN TRIUMPHANT."

THE SECRETARY. The vote in the army was almost unanimous for Lincoln. The Tycoon sent over the first fruits of victory to the Hell-Cat and went to work shoveling out fried oysters.

THE GUIDE. The almighty must have stuffed the ballot-boxes!

THE SOLDIER. Give Uncle Abe my compliments!

(All but **MCCLELLAN** *exit. MUSIC under: "MARCHING ALONG," slowly.)*

MCCLELLAN. I have the honor to resign my commission as a Major General in the Army of the U.S.A. I think that we have well played our parts. The mistakes made were not of our making – and before the curtain falls I trust that we will see they were a part of the grand plan of the Almighty, who designed that the cup should be drained even to the bitter dregs, that the people might be made worthy of being saved.

(Music ends. **MCCLELLAN** *executes a smart about-face and exits.)*

> *PROJECTION (56):*
> *GENERAL WILLIAM T.*
> *SHERMAN, LOOKING*
> *VERY MUCH LIKE AN*
> *OLD TESTAMENT PROPHET.*

*(***THE GUIDE*** *steps into the light.)*

THE GUIDE. "They could have had a hundred years of peace and prosperity, but they preferred war. Very well. Last year they could have saved their slaves, but now it is too late. Next, their lands will be taken; and in another year they may beg in vain for their lives. Prepare them for my coming. General William T. Sherman."

(Footlights up. With a joyous whoop **THE SOLDIER** *runs on, carrying his rifle, bayonet shoved into his belt.)*

THE SOLDIER.

BRING THE GOOD OLD BUGLE, BOYS, WE'LL SING ANOTHER SONG.
SING IT WITH A SPIRIT THAT WILL START THE WORLD ALONG.

SING IT LIKE WE USED TO SING IT, FIFTY THOUSAND
   STRONG,
WHILE WE WERE MARCHING THROUGH GEORGIA.

(**THE FREEDMAN** *enters with rifle and bayonet and joins him.* **THE SECRETARY**, **THE GUIDE & THE HOMETOWN GIRL** *stand on the edges of the stage, joining in the chorus.*)

ALL.

HURRAH! HURRAH! WE BRING THE JUBILEE!
HURRAH! HURRAH! THE FLAG THAT MAKES YOU FREE!
SO WE SANG THE CHORUS FROM ATLANTA TO THE
   SEA,
WHILE WE WERE MARCHING THROUGH GEORGIA.

PROJECTION (57):
CLOSE-UP OF
SHERMAN'S FACE.

(**THE FREEDMAN & THE SOLDIER** *fix bayonets to their rifles.*)

THE GUIDE. "War is cruelty. There is no use trying to reform it. The crueler it is, the sooner it will be over."

THE SOLDIER.

SO WE MADE A THOROUGHFARE FOR FREEDOM AND
   HER TRAIN,

THE FREEDMAN.

SIXTY MILES IN LATITUDE, THREE HUNDRED TO THE
   MAIN.

THE SOLDIER.

TREASON FLED BEFORE US,

THE FREEDMAN.

FOR RESISTANCE WAS IN VAIN,

BOTH.

WHILE WE WERE MARCHING THROUGH GEORGIA.

ALL.

> HURRAH! HURRAH! WE BRING THE JUBILEE!
> HURRAH! HURRAH! THE FLAG THAT MAKES YOU FREE.
> SO WE SANG THE CHORUS FROM ATLANTA TO THE
>   SEA,
> WHILE WE WERE MARCHING THROUGH GEORGIA.

> > *PROJECTION (58):*
> > *EXTREME CLOSE-UP*
> > *OF SHERMAN'S EYES.*

THE GUIDE. "Mr. President: I beg to present you as a Christmas gift, the city of Savannah. The whole army is burning to wreak vengeance upon South Carolina. I almost tremble at her fate."

> > *PROJECTION (59):*
> > *THE RUINS OF*
> > *CHARLESTON.*

*(The music has turned mournful. The two **SOL-DIERS** wield their bayonets in a slow-motion destructive frenzy.)*

ALL.

> HURRAH! HURRAH! WE BRING THE JUBILEE!
> HURRAH! HURRAH! THE FLAG THAT MAKES YOU FREE.
> SO WE SANG THE CHORUS FROM ATLANTA TO THE
>   SEA,
> WHILE WE WERE MARCHING THROUGH GEORGIA.

(As the music ends, the stage is plunged into blackness. All exit.)

> > *PROJECTION (60):*
> > *PORTRAIT OF*
> > *JOHN WILKES BOOTH.*

BOOTH (HAWK). *(offstage)* Abe must die, and now. We trust some bold hand will pierce his heart with dagger point for the public good.

(MUSIC: "HAIL TO THE CHIEF.")

PROJECTION (61):
| "FORD'S THEATRE
PRESENTS JOHN WILKES
BOOTH IN 'THE APOSTATE'. "

(Theatre box as before, **THE SECRETARY** *positioned as before.* **JOHN WILKES BOOTH (HAWK)** *enters in a dark cloak and plumed hat costumed for a role.)*

THE SECRETARY. The Hell-cat invited us to Ford's Theatre. John Wilkes Booth played the villain. Twice during the play, Booth came very near to our box, thrust his finger at the Tycoon and uttered extremely disagreeable threats. When he did it a third time...

*(***BOOTH*** thrusts out a warning finger toward the box.)*

BOOTH (HAWK).
"If you detest me as the serpent's coil,
Fear – fear me as its sting! My lifted hand
Holds death above thy head."

(He stalks upstage as if to his dressing room, removing his hat.)

THE SECRETARY. *(concerned)* I said, "Mr. President, he looks as if he meant that for you!" The Tycoon laughed. "Well," he said, "he does look pretty sharp at me, doesn't he?" After the play, the Tycoon asked to meet Booth...

BOOTH. *(the vilest insult he can muster)* I would rather have the applause of a Negro.

(He exits.)

THE SECRETARY. *(puzzled)* But he received no reply.

*(***THE FREEDMAN*** enters.)*

THE FREEDMAN. From Lieutenant General Grant: "I mean to end the business here."

(Blackout.)

PROJECTION (62):
AN ARMY FIELD
SURGEON WITH SAW
IN HAND, PREPARING
FOR AN AMPUTATION.

(Lights up on **THE SOLDIER** *propped up on his knapsack as a pillow.* **THE NURSE** *is at his side. She is completely spent.)*

THE NURSE. We have been two days in the field. There is a great want of surgeons here. We have some plucky boys in the hospital, but they suffer awfully.

(She starts to exit, turns back wearily.)

I do not know when I shall go home – it will be according to how long this hospital stays here and whether another battle comes soon. I feel assured I shall never feel horrified at anything that may happen to me hereafter.

(She exits. **THE SOLDIER** *speaks, through the haze and confusion of morphine.)*

THE SOLDIER. Suddenly, the rebel infantry opened upon us. I had fired a dozen rounds when my left foot, of its own accord, raised from the ground, and I felt the hot blood streaming down my thigh. The pain was so acute that I grew deathly sick; everything faded from my sight, and sense left me.

(As projection fades out, **THE NURSE** *appears back-lit through a scrim. She is draped in white, an angelic vision arising from* **THE SOLDIER** *'s morphine-induced confusion.)*

THE NURSE.
BEAUTIFUL DREAMER, WAKE UNTO ME,
STARLIGHT AND DEWDROPS ARE WAITING FOR THEE;
SOUNDS OF THE RUDE WORLD HEARD IN THE DAY,
LULL'D BY THE MOONLIGHT, HAVE ALL PASSED AWAY!

THE SOLDIER. But I soon awoke. Where was I? I had been laid upon the ground near a small school-house where the work of amputation was going on...

THE NURSE.
GONE ARE THE CARES OF LIFE'S BUSY THRONG,
BEAUTIFUL DREAMER, AWAKE UNTO ME!

THE SOLDIER. I lay the whole afternoon outside the schoolhouse, listening to the horrible screams which came from within and, to kill time, gazing upon a heap of men's arms and legs piled up against the side of the house.

THE NURSE.
BEAUTIFUL DREAMER, OUT ON THE SEA,
MERMAIDS ARE CHANTING THE WILD LORELEI;

THE SOLDIER. It was near evening when my turn came. I was carried in and laid upon the operating table....

THE NURSE.
BEAUTIFUL DREAMER, BEAM ON MY HEART,
E'EN AS THE MORN ON THE STREAMLET AND SEA;
THEN WILL ALL CLOUDS OF SORROW DEPART,
BEAUTIFUL DREAMER, AWAKE UNTO ME!
BEAUTIFUL DREAMER, AWAKE UNTO ME!

THE SOLDIER. "Tell me, doctor, must my leg be amputated?" He thrust his finger into the wound....

THE NURSE. *(tenderly)* That bone is shivered all to pieces; and if you value your life....

THE SOLDIER. *(calmly)* I said no more. Chloroform was administered; I sank into unconsciousness; and when I awoke – it was all over.

BOTH.
THEN WILL ALL CLOUDS OF SORROW DEPART!
BEAUTIFUL DREAMER, AWAKE UNTO ME!

(Lights fade on **THE SOLDIER**.*)*

THE NURSE.

BEAUTIFUL DREAMER, AWAKE UNTO ME!

(Lights fade to black.)

> PROJECTION (63):
> THE BURNT-OUT
> RUINS OF RICHMOND.

*(***THE SECRETARY*** *enters.)*

THE FREEDMAN. "From Lieutenant General Grant: The rebels have evacuated Richmond. If the thing is pressed, I think that Lee will surrender."

THE SECRETARY. *(dictates)* "From the President. Lieutenant General Grant: Let the thing be pressed."

(Drumroll: the long roll. Drums continue under dialogue.)

> PROJECTION (64):
> "SURRENDER OF
> GENERAL LEE."

THE FREEDMAN. Lee's army moved forward into gray columns. The old swaying battle-flags were crowded so thick, by thinning out of men, that the whole column seemed crowned with red.

THE SECRETARY. Was not such manhood to be welcomed back into a Union so tested and assured?

THE FREEDMAN. And now only the flag of the Union greets the sky.

THE SECRETARY. When the news reached him, all Mr. Lincoln said was, "Thank God I have lived to see this."

(Drumroll ends.)

"The nightmare is over."

*(***THE SECRETARY*** *exits into office,* **THE FREEDWOMAN** *enters,* **THE FREEDMAN** *crosses to her.* **HAWK** *enters. He is now dressed as the rube Asa Trenchard in "Our American Cousin," but speaks as himself.)*

HAWK. The day was a pleasant one throughout the whole land. There were many lilacs in full bloom. But the evening turned cold, raw, and gusty. Dark clouds enveloped the capital.

> *PROJECTION (65):*
> *"OUR AMERICAN*
> *COUSIN" PLAYBILL.*

HAWK. *(cont.)* Inside, the theatre was crowded, cheerful – with perfumes, music of violins and flutes.

(MUSIC in: "Hail to the Chief.")

> *PROJECTION (66):*
> *CAST LIST, WITH*
> *THE NAME "MR.*
> *HARRY HAWK"*
> *HIGHLIGHTED.)*

(Footlights up, and **HAWK** *and* **MRS. MUZZY (CORDELIA)** *take their places as* **ACTORS** *in "Our American Cousin.")*

Mrs. Muzzy turned to me….

MRS. MUZZY (CORDELIA). *(witheringly)* "I am aware, Mr. Trenchard, you are not used to the manners of good society, and that, alone, will excuse the impertinence of which you have been guilty."

(She sails off with an imperious flourish of her fan. **HAWK** *continues broadly, as the character Asa Trenchard.)*

HAWK. *(slyly)* "Well, I guess I know enough to turn you inside out, old gal – you sockdologizing old man-trap!"

(He stands for a moment, listening for the remembered outburst of laughter. When he resumes, he has dropped the comic character.)

HAWK. *(cont.)* I was looking up at the President's box – the words had barely left my lips, and the shouts of laughter were ringing, when the shot sounded through the house....

BOOTH (TRUDGETT). *(offstage shout)* Sic semper tyrannis!

*(**HAWK** wrestles with his own memory of the night Lincoln was killed. As he recounts the story, **COMPANY MEMBERS** perform snatches of the action behind him in shafts of light.)*

HAWK. NO!! No! There was no shout! A man leapt down to the stage. I saw his left foot crumple under him. He was rushing towards me with a dagger – I could feel his breath – and I turned and ran upstage. The hundreds in the audience had not the least idea of what was happening. They all thought it was part of the play! I turned back and – My God! That's John Booth! *Then* there was a shout –

HANNIBAL. *(off)* Stop that man!

HAWK. Mrs. Lincoln cried out. There was absolute quiet except for Mrs. Lincoln's voice. I couldn't tell what she was trying to say – no one could. She continued to call for a long time –

TRUDGETT. *(shouted, offstage)* For God's sake, what happened?

HANNIBAL. *(shouted, offstage)* He shot the President!

HAWK. And then the deluge. They climbed over the footlights and poured onto the stage. Women fainted. We actors stood there in our painted faces, with mortal fright showing through the rouge. The soldiers burst in – they charged the audience with fixed bayonets, shouting –

HAWK & HANNIBAL. Clear out! Clear out! You sons of –

HAWK. The man they were after had fled through the stage door. Laura Keene rushed out from the wing...

*(***LAURA KEENE (CORDELIA)*** enters and rushes to the edge of the stage, pleading directly with the audience)*

LAURA KEENE (CORDELIA). *(calling out)* For God's sake, keep your places, and all will be well!

(She exits.)

HAWK. The memory of that apparition will never leave me. It was John Booth. I could say it if I was on my deathbed. In the midst of that pandemonium, the life blood from those veins dripped slowly down. And as they carried the President from the theatre, I stood alone on the stage once more.

(He stands for a moment, not sure what to do. **HAN-NIBAL** *crosses to him, taking him gently by the arm, and leads him offstage.* **THE FREEDWOMAN** *and* **THE NURSE** *enter and meet center.)*

THE FREEDWOMAN. The streets were suddenly crowded with people.

THE NURSE. The President still lived.

*(***THE SECRETARY*** bursts in through the office door.)*

THE SECRETARY. A crowd rushed to the White House and bursting through the doors, shouted the dreadful news to us. I ran downstairs, found a carriage at the door and drove to Tenth Street. By then, I was prepared for the worst. I watched at his bed through the night. At twenty-two minutes past seven, a look of unspeakable peace came upon his worn features.

(Music: bells.)

THE NURSE. The tolling of the bells announced that he had ceased to breathe.

THE SECRETARY. Mr. Stanton broke the silence: "Now he belongs to the ages."

(**THE FREEDWOMAN** *and* **THE NURSE** *draw their shawls over their heads. Lights down.* **THE FREED-MAN & THE SOLDIER** *move to Lincoln's empty theater chair. They drape it with a black shroud, lift it solemnly and carry the "bier" slowly to center, where they place it and salute as a military funeral escort.* **THE FREEDMAN** *sings.*)

THE FREEDMAN.
STEAL AWAY,
STEAL AWAY,
STEAL AWAY TO JESUS.

(*Music continues under.*)

THE FREEDMAN.
STEAL AWAY,
STEAL AWAY HOME.
I AIN'T GOT LONG
TO STAY HERE.

THE SOLDIER.
What a hold old Honest Abe Lincoln had on the hearts of the soldiers. Just before the funeral procession began to move, the Twenty-Second U.S. Colored Infantry landed from Petersburg and marched up to a position on the avenue. When the head of the column came up, they played a dirge, and headed the procession to the Capitol.

(**THE SECRETARY** *appears on the set's highest level. Music continues under.*)

THE FREEDMAN.

STEAL AWAY,
STEAL AWAY,
STEAL AWAY TO JESUS.
STEAL AWAY,
STEAL AWAY HOME.
I AIN'T GOT LONG
TO STAY HERE.

THE SECRETARY.

While they were passing, I went alone up the winding stairs to the top of the great dome. Directly beneath me lay the casket in which the dead President lay at full length, far, far below. And like black atoms moving over a sheet of gray paper, the slow-moving mourners crept silently across the rotunda.

(Music continues as he crosses down to the floor level.)

PROJECTION (67):
THE FUNERAL PROGRAM.

THE FREEDMAN.

MY LORD CALLS ME,
HE CALLS ME BY THE
    LIGHTNING!
THE TRUMPET
    SOUNDS WITHIN
    MY SOUL,
I AIN'T GOT LONG
    TO STAY HERE.

THE FREEDMAN.
STEAL AWAY
THE FREEDWOMAN.
(STEAL AWAY)
THE FREEDMAN.
STEAL AWAY
THE FREEDWOMAN.
(STEAL AWAY)
BOTH.
STEAL AWAY TO
JESUS.
THE FREEDMAN.
STEAL AWAY
THE FREEDWOMAN.
(STEAL AWAY)

THE SECRETARY.
The funeral train passed over the same route we had taken East. Thousands of the plain people he loved came out from their homes to stand bareheaded as the train swept by, its westward progress through the night marked by campfires built along the course.

THE NURSE.
When lilacs last in the dooryard bloomed,
And the great star early drooped in the western sky in the night,
I mourned, and yet shall mourn with ever-returning spring.
Here, coffin that slowly passes...

THE FREEDMAN & THE FREEDWOMAN.
STEAL AWAY HOME.

(**THE SECRETARY** crosses to the bier.)

THE SECRETARY. I give you my sprig of lilac.

THE FREEDMAN & THE FREEDWOMAN.
I AIN'T GOT LONG TO STAY HERE.

(Sound of a low, keening train whistle fades into the distance as lights fade on the bier. All exit. **HAWK** enters and sings simply, directly to the audience.)

HAWK.

> LET US PAUSE IN LIFE'S PLEASURES AND COUNT ITS
> MANY TEARS,
> WHILE WE ALL SUP SORROW WITH THE POOR.
> THERE'S A SONG THAT WILL LINGER FOREVER IN OUR
> EARS:
> OH! HARD TIMES, COME AGAIN NO MORE.
> 'TIS THE SONG, THE SIGH OF THE WEARY:
> HARD TIMES, HARD TIMES, COME AGAIN NO MORE!
> MANY DAYS YOU HAVE LINGERED AROUND MY CABIN
> DOOR,
> OH! HARD TIMES, COME AGAIN NO MORE.

> *(Music continues under.* **CORDELIA** *enters.)*

CORDELIA. So the army returned to Washington, to the banks of the river whose name and fame they bore, flowing in darkness past them, as from dream to dream. And it must be that by such things as we had seen and done and suffered, a step is taken in the homeward march of man.

HAWK.

> OH! HARD TIMES, COME AGAIN NO MORE.

HAWK & CORDELIA.

> 'TIS A SIGH THAT IS WAFTED ACROSS THE TROUBLED
> WAVE,
> 'TIS A WAIL THAT IS HEARD UPON THE SHORE –

> *(Music continues under as* **TRUDGETT** *enters.)*

TRUDGETT. I could smell the ham cooking, and the coffee – it made me hungry clean down to my toes. After doing full justice to the breakfast, I took off the old army blue and put on the citizen clothes and went down to the saw mill. I filed the saw and started the old saw mill and made the saw dust fly. And I would do it all again if they should want three hundred thousand more.

HAWK, CORDELIA & TRUDGETT.

OH! HARD TIMES, COME AGAIN NO MORE.
'TIS A DIRGE THAT IS MURMURED AROUND THE
    LOWLY GRAVE:
OH! HARD TIMES, COME AGAIN NO MORE.

(Music continues under as **LOVECRAFT** *enters.)*

LOVECRAFT. "We must believe that our Heavenly Father permits this war for some wise purpose of his own, mysterious and unknown to us; and though we may not be able to comprehend it, yet we cannot but believe that he who made the world still governs it." Abraham Lincoln.

HAWK, CORDELIA, TRUDGETT & LOVECRAFT.

OH! HARD TIMES, COME AGAIN NO MORE.
WHILE WE SEEK MIRTH AND BEAUTY
AND MUSIC LIGHT AND GAY,
THERE ARE FRAIL FORMS FAINTING AT THE DOOR.
THOUGH THEIR VOICES ARE SILENT,
THEIR PLEADING LOOKS WILL SAY:
"OH! HARD TIMES, COME AGAIN NO MORE."

(Music changes as **CASSIE** *enters.)*

CASSIE. I purchased my tickets via railroad. I did not wait for the stage, but we started on foot. The next day I found my daughter grown to womanhood. I turned my face again to the North, my daughter, her husband and child coming with me. Three times since, I made the same journey, bringing back with me in all sixteen of my relatives.

(**HANNIBAL** *joins her.*)

HANNIBAL. To our old Master: I was glad to find that you wanted us to come back to live with you again. We have concluded to test your sincerity by asking you to send our wages for the time we served you. With interest, our earnings would amount to eleven thousand, six hundred and eighty dollars.

CASSIE. *(warmly)* Say howdy to George Carter.

HANNIBAL. And thank him for taking the pistol from you when you were shooting at me. Your *former* servants, Hannibal and Cassandra Drumwright.

COMPANY.
'TIS THE SONG, THE SIGH OF THE WEARY:
HARD TIMES, HARD TIMES, COME AGAIN NO MORE!
MANY DAYS YOU HAVE LINGERED AROUND MY CABIN
DOOR!
OH! HARD TIMES, COME AGAIN NO MORE.
OH! HARD TIMES, COME AGAIN NO MORE.

(*Lights fade to black.*)

The End

ALTERNATE OPENING FOR EXPANDED CAST VERSION

(House lights dim. A drumroll, a trumpet fan-fare, and a spotlight. The act curtain lurches open to reveal **HARRY HAWK**, *a down-at-the-heels actor-manager accompanied by his indispensable stage manager and alter ego,* **HANNIBAL DRUM-WRIGHT**.*)*

HAWK. Distinguished patrons of the lyceum! I welcome you this evening with a deep sense of occasion, for it is a quarter of a century to the day – indeed, almost to the hour – since I found myself center stage in the tragic drama that shook the republic to its very foundations. Permit me to introduce myself – Harry Hawk: actor, manager – one might even say impresario of our wandering band. Tonight, we have the great honor to present the story of the late war to save the Union, woven from the very words of those engaged in that heroic struggle, bedecked with the never-to-be-forgotten melodies of those tempest-tossed years, and illuminated by the astonishing wonders of – The Magic Lantern!

(A triumphant chord from the orchestra, and an elaborately ornate hand-tinted projection (#1) appears upstage:)

> *MR. HARRY HAWK'S*
> *COMPANY PRESENTS*
> *"REUNION!"*
> *THE AMERICAN ILIAD!*

*(***HAWK*** *continues grandly.)*

For the past quarter of a century, we have played our drama before the Great and the near-Great, the very stage itself bursting to hold our army of actors and the sheer extravagance of our production!

(He comes back to reality.)

HAWK. *(cont.)* Unhappily, you find us in somewhat diminished circumstances, as a regrettable misunderstanding with certain of our less imaginative creditors has dictated the hasty withdrawal of our forces from the field of our latest triumph. It pains me to announce that in the chaos of retreat, not all of our brave number escaped.

(He brightens.)

But happily, our ranks have been reinforced thanks to the abundance of gifted amateurs to be found in…

(He is at a loss to remember where the company has landed.)

…your fair city!

*(With a sweeping gesture, **HAWK** summons the entire ragtag **COMPANY** on stage, in varying stages of readiness. He holds his breath as his untried troops execute this first crucial maneuver with a minimum of damage to themselves or the set. As a relieved **HAWK** prepares to continue, the young actor who will play **THE SOLDIER** trips noisily on, perhaps sacrificing some small piece of scenery as he does. He smiles winningly.)*

Ah, well! In the deathless words of Homer, "Surely these things lie in the lap of the gods." Therefore – tonight, we shall appear in many roles, asking only that you unfetter your imaginations as you journey with us. In the fervent hope that you shall deem us worthy of your approbation, I give you our musical epic… in miniature.

(After a deep bow, he exits. Blackout. Footlights up on male minstrel trio.)

PROP LIST

ACT ONE
6 light chairs movable by actors, or more if larger cast is used (Company)
Trunks as needed (Company)
Wardrobe baskets as needed (Company)
Book (Abolitionist)
Lantern (Guide)
Pistol (Guide)
Lincoln campaign pins (New Yorkers)
Stack of mail (Secretary)
Bunting for theatre box
Lincoln's chair
Stack of newspapers (Newsboy)
Rifle (Soldier)
Blue Regimental flag (Patriotic Girl)
Written speech (Patriotic Girl)
Prop rifles (Music Hall Zouaves)
Valise (Nurse)
Photo case (Nurse)
Broadsword (Actor)
Telegram (Porter)
Camp chair (McClellan)
Fans (Washington Ladies)
Knapsack (Soldier)
Whiskey jug (Soldier)
Bible (Temperance Lady)
3 cigars wrapped in a dispatch (Soldier)
Duplicate dispatch (McClellan)
2 identical newspapers (Freedman, McClellan)
Rifle (Freedman)

ACT TWO
Beer stein (Waitress)
String of sausages (Butcher)
Meat cleaver (Butcher)
Stiff dog leash with collar (Immigrant Boy)
Wash basin (Nurse)
Bandages (Nurse)
Cane (Widow)
White hanky (Widow)
Wad of bills (Substitute Broker)
Paper and pen (Patriotic Girl)
Paper and pencil (Soldiers)
2 photo cases (Patriotic Girl, Soldier)
Knapsacks (Soldiers)
Rifles (Soldiers)
Pins (Soldiers)

2 newspapers (Freedman & Secretary)
Letter (Secretary)
Dispatch (Guide)
Bayonets (Soldiers)
Fan (Mrs. Muzzy)
Black shroud (Soldier & Freedman)

COSTUME PLOT

(for 6-actor cast)

Each actor has a basic costume. Except for a handful of more elaborate pieces such as the music hall scenes or Hawk's transformation to McClellan, the play works best when changes occur by the simple addition or subtraction of a piece or two, and often in view of the audience. Unless noted otherwise, pieces listed are added to the actor's basic costume. Decisions about under-dressing pieces will vary depending on the theatre's situation.

HARRY HAWK

ACT ONE

Basic costume: Waistcoat, dark blue pants, white shirt, cravat, low black boots

Harry Hawk, top of show: Add frock coat, top hat

Minstrel: Striped tailcoat and top hat

New Yorker: Frock coat

Secessionist: Frock coat, white broad-brimmed planter's hat

Actor: Toga

Farewell Committee: Frock coat, top hat, mayor's sash

Music Hall Performer: Zouave uniform blouse, cap

Actor: Gold crown, Shakespearean doublet, riding boots

McClellan: Union General's frock coat, riding boots, chasseur cap or kepi (called a "McClellan cap")

ACT TWO

Harry Hawk: Frock coat, riding boots

Butcher: Butcher's apron, riding boots

McClellan: Union General's frock coat, riding boots, McClellan cap

Music Hall Widow: Mother Hubbard and bonnet, granny glasses, riding boots under

McClellan: Union General's frock coat, riding boots, McClellan cap

John Wilkes Booth: Cloak and plumed hat

Harry Hawk: "Rube" frock coat and hat ("Our American Cousin")

Harry Hawk, Finale: Basic costume

AUGUSTIN LOVECRAFT

ACT ONE

Basic costume: Waistcoat, black/dark grey
pants, white shirt, cravat, black shoes
Augustin Lovecraft, top of show: Black/
dark grey frock coat
Minstrel: Striped tailcoat and top hat
New Yorker: Frock coat
Secretary: Frock coat, overcoat, top hat,
glasses
Farewell Committee: Frock coat, top hat
Music Hall Performer: Zouave uniform
blouse, cap
Secretary: Frock coat, glasses
Irish Tenor: Derby, green waistcoat,
swallowtail coat
Secretary: Frock coat, glasses

ACT TWO

Secretary: Frock coat, glasses
Soldier: Union soldier blouse, cap
(Soldier)
Secretary: Frock coat, glasses
Augustin Lovecraft, Finale: Frock
coat

CORDELIA HOPEWELL

ACT ONE

Basic costume: White blouse, cameo,
skirt, shoes
Cordelia Hopewell, top of show: Fancy
hat, [TOP], traveling cape
Abolitionist: Basic costume
Northern Spy: Hat, shawl
Washington Lady: Basic costume
Patriotic Girl: Shawl
Music Hall Performer: "Zouave" show-
girl costume, tights, boots
Nurse: Traveling cloak, bonnet
Washington Lady: Basic costume
Temperance Lady: Black blouse or
shawl, black bonnet, glasses
Nurse: Basic costume
Nurse: Blood-spattered apron
Nurse: Basic costume

ACT TWO

Music Hall Waitress: Dirndl dress,
tights, blond pigtail wig
Nurse: Basic costume, apron
Hometown Girl: Basic costume
McClellan Supporter: Basic
costume
Nurse: Basic costume, blood-
spattered aprol
Nurse/Angelic Vision: White chif-
fon drape
Mrs. Muzzy: Frilly lace cap
Laura Keen, Nurse: Dark shawl
Cordelia Hopewell, Finale: Basic
costume

TOM TRUDGETT

ACT ONE

Basic costume: White shirt, light blue pants, black cravat, dark suspenders, low boots.

Tom Trudgett, top of show: Basic costume

Minstrel: Striped tailcoat, top hat

New Yorker: Frock coat

Newsboy: Basic costume

Soldier, Sentry: Union private's blouse, belt, cap, private stripe

Soldier: change private stripe to corporal's stripes

ACT TWO

Music Hall Immigrant Boy: Brown lederhosen, white shirt, red suspenders, green Bavarian hat with feather, knee socks, boots

Soldier: Basic costume with Union soldier blouse, belt, cap, corporal's stripes

Music Hall Draftee: Oversized uniform coat and cap

Soldier: Union soldier's blouse, belt, cap, sergeant's stripes

Tom Trudgett, Finale: Basic costume

HANNIBAL DRUMWRIGHT

ACT ONE

Basic costume: White shirt, waistcoat, cravat, suspenders, dark pants, low boots

Hannibal Drumwright, top of show: Frock coat

Fugitive Slave: Basic costume, remove waistcoat and cravat

New Yorker: Frock coat, restore waistcoat and cravat

Freedman: Dark frock coat

Porter, Hannibal: Basic costume

Madame Duprez' Saloonkeeper: Derby and sleeve garters

Freedman: Dark frock coat

Hannibal: Basic costume

Freedman: Dark frock coat

Hannibal: Basic costume

Freedman: Dark frock coat

Freedman: Union soldier blouse, belt, cap, private's stripe

ACT TWO

Hannibal: Basic costume

Music Hall Substitute Broker: Checkered waistcoat, Derby and sleeve garters

Freedman: Union soldier blouse, belt, cap, corporal's stripes

Hannibal: Basic costume

Freedman: Union soldier blouse, belt, cap, sergeant's stripes

Hannibal Drumwright, Finale: Basic costume

CASSIE DRUMWRIGHT

ACT ONE

Basic costume: White blouse, skirt, shoes

Cassandra Drumwright, top of show: Hat, cloak

Underground Railroad Guide: Slouch hat, riding coat

New Yorker: Jacket, hat

Maid: Apron

Freedwoman: Elegant hat with feather, brocade jacket

Guide: Slouch hat, riding coat

Guide: Remove hat, coat

ACT TWO

Freedwoman: Basic costume

Guide: Slouch hat, riding coat

Freedwoman: Basic costume, add dark shawl

Cassandra Drumwright, Finale: Basic costume

SOUND EFFECTS

ACT ONE
1. Before Lincoln & Liberty: Crowd in large auditorium
2. Secretary leaves Springfield: Train whistle quick blasts
3. Soldier's farewell: Train whistle quick blasts
4. Nurse arrives in Washington: Train whistle
5. After We'll Fight for Uncle Abe: Battle sounds (cannon fire, bugle calls, horses, etc.)

ACT TWO
1. McClellan's farewell: Train whistle
2. McClellan's farewell: Train whistle
3. Lincoln's funeral: Train whistle fading into distance

OTHER TITLES AVAILABLE FROM SAMUEL FRENCH

ABE

Book and Lyrics by Lee Goldsmith
Music by Roger Anderson

Musical / 16m, 9f

Abe is a new musical about the early life of Abraham Lincoln. The show explores his youth as a flatboat pilot on the Mississippi, his early love for Ann Rutledge, his troubled marriage to the difficult and mentally fragile Mary Todd, and his attempt to be a good father to his sons. The story follows Abe from his earliest attempts at self-improvement through the 1860 election which made him the 16th president of an already fracturing United States.

The score is fully orchestrated and uses bold, melodic and traditional musical theatre styles that embrace the story's period and Americana roots. It can be produced fully staged or as a concert performance. The musical features a large cast and requires strong singers: baritone, soprano, mezzo-soprano, 3 adult male singing roles, 3 male children singing roles, male/female chorus with many speaking roles.

"The founding fathers got their own musical with 1776, so why not Abe?"
- Playbill.com

OTHER TITLES AVAILABLE FROM SAMUEL FRENCH

AMERICAN TALES

Book and Lyrics by Ken Stone
Music by Jan Powell

Musical in two acts, based on stories by classic American writers / 4m, 1f

Ovation Award nomination for Best Book/Lyrics/Music
Kleban Award winner, Libretto (Bartleby, the Scrivener)

Act I, The Loves of Alonzo Fitz Clarence and Rosannah Ethelton, is from Mark Twain's story of two people falling in love at a great distance with the aid of that brand-new invention, the telephone. Alonzo in Maine and Rosannah in California meet by the accident of crossed wires and each falls in love with an imagined ideal of the other. So complete is their self-deception that even when brought face to face they cannot recognize each other. Love is found, lost, and found again. Played as period melodrama, but the relevance to 21st century dating habits is clear.

Act II, Bartleby, the Scrivener, is dramatized from Herman Melville's slyly funny but ultimately tragic story. Building on the theme of human connections made and missed, this act takes a darker turn, looking at people who occupy the closest of quarters and yet don't really communicate at all. Bartleby, employed as a copyist in a law office of the 1840s, inexplicably begins to refuse to work, forcing his colleagues to ask themselves the transforming question that ends the play: What do we owe to the people who come into our lives?

"Excellent new musical."
- Critic's Choice, LA Times

"Extraordinary...skillful and unusually thoughtful...succeeds brilliantly."
- Variety

"Marvelous adaptations ... stylish and enthralling ... haunting score ... brilliant."
- Critic's Pick, Backstage

"Striking ... absolutely first rate work."
- EDGE Los Angeles
SAMUELFRENCH.COM

OTHER TITLES AVAILABLE FROM SAMUEL FRENCH

THE MIDNIGHT RIDE OF PAUL REVERE

Book and Lyrics by Ben H. Winters
Music and Lyrics by Stephen Sislen

5m, 1f, with doubling, expandable cast / Unit Set

In Boston, Paul Revere etches out a humble living as a silver-smith. Americans and British alike hail the exquisite artistry of his work. But when Paul's revolutionary friends, John Hancock and Samuel Adams pressure Revere to take a stand against British tyranny and join the Sons of Liberty, he worries that supporting the cause of revolution would mean losing his business and risking the safety of his family. Revere must make a choice: to do what is easy, or to do what is right. From the halls of British Parliament, to the port of Boston and the "Tea Party" protest, to the Boston Massacre and the dangerous thrill of Revere's now-legendary ride, this new musical makes American history accessible and exciting through a unique combination of music, drama and humor. *The Midnight Ride of Paul Revere* tells the inspirational, universal story of how ordinary people can make a difference.